Teggs is no ordinary dinosaur –
he's an **ASTROSAUR!** Captain of
the amazing spaceship DSS *Sauropod*,
he goes on dangerous missions and
fights evil – along with his faithful
crew, Gipsy, Arx and Iggy.

For more astro-fun visit the website
www.astrosaurs.co.uk

Read all the adventures of
Teggs, Gipsy, Arx and Iggy!

RIDDLE OF THE RAPTORS
THE HATCHING HORROR
THE SEAS OF DOOM
THE MIND-SWAP MENACE
THE SKIES OF FEAR
THE SPACE GHOSTS
DAY OF THE DINO-DROIDS
THE TERROR-BIRD TRAP
THE PLANET OF PERIL
THE STAR PIRATES
THE CLAWS OF CHRISTMAS
THE SUN-SNATCHERS
REVENGE OF THE FANG
THE CARNIVORE CURSE
THE DREAMS OF DREAD
THE ROBOT RAIDERS
THE TWIST OF TIME
THE SABRE-TOOTH SECRET
THE FOREST OF EVIL

Also available by the same author,
these fantastic series:

Cows in Action
Astrosaurs
Astrosaurs Academy
SLIME SQUAD

Find out more at www.stevecolebooks.co.uk

Astrosaurs

MEGABOOKASAURUS!

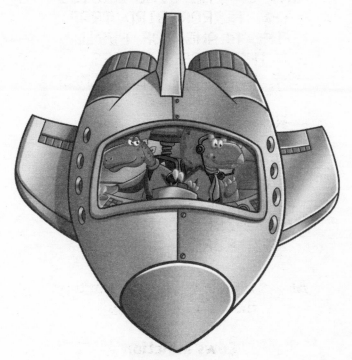

Steve Cole

Illustrated by Charlie Fowkes and Woody Fox

RED FOX

MEGABOOKASAURUS
A RED FOX BOOK 978 1 849 41553 8

Collection first published in Great Britain by Red Fox, an imprint of
Random House Children's Books. A Random House Company

First Red Fox Edition published 2009. This edition published 2011

1 3 5 7 9 10 8 6 4 2

THE HATCHING HORROR
First published in Great Britain by Red Fox, 2005

THE MIND-SWAP MENACE
First published in Great Britain by Red Fox, 2005

TEETH OF THE T.REX
First published in Great Britain by Red Fox, 2007

The Random House Group Limited supports the Forest Stewardship Council® (FSC®),
the leading international forest certification organisation. All our titles that are printed on
Greenpeace approved FSC® certified paper carry the FSC® logo. Our paper procurement
policy can be found at www.randomhouse.co.uk/environment

MIX
Paper from
responsible sources
FSC® C016897

Red Fox Books are published by Random House Children's Books,
61–63 Uxbridge Road, London W5 5SA

www.kidsatrandomhouse.co.uk   www.totallyrandombooks.co.uk   www.randomhouse.co.uk

Addresses for companies within The Random House Group Limited can be found at:
www.randomhouse.co.uk/offices.htm

THE RANDOM HOUSE GROUP Limited Reg. No. 954009

A CIP catalogue record for this book is available from the British Library.

Printed and bound in Great Britain by CPI Bookmarque, Croydon, CR0 4TD

WARNING!

THINK YOU KNOW ABOUT DINOSAURS?

THINK AGAIN!

The dinosaurs . . .

Big, stupid, lumbering reptiles. Right?

All they did was eat, sleep and roar a bit. Right?

Died out millions of years ago when a big meteor struck the Earth. Right?

Wrong!

The dinosaurs weren't stupid. They
may have had small brains, but they
used them well. They had big thoughts
and big dreams.

By the time the meteor hit, the last
dinosaurs had already left Earth for
ever. Some breeds had discovered how
to travel through space as early as
the Triassic period, and were already
enjoying a new life among the stars.
No one has found evidence of dinosaur
technology yet. But the first fossil bones
were only unearthed in 1822, and new
finds are being made all the time.

The proof is out there, buried in the
ground.

And the dinosaurs live on, way out in
space, even now. They've settled down in
a place they call the Jurassic Quadrant
and over the last sixty-five million years
they've gone on evolving.

The dinosaurs we'll be meeting are

 part of a special group called the Dinosaur Space Service. Their job is to explore space, to go on exciting missions and to fight evil and protect the innocent!

These heroic herbivores are not just dinosaurs.

They are *astrosaurs*!

NOTE: The following story has been translated from secret Dinosaur Space Service records. Earthling dinosaur names are used throughout, although some changes have been made for easy reading. There's even a guide to help you pronounce the dinosaur names on the next page.

THE CREW OF THE DSS SAUROPOD

**CAPTAIN
TEGGS STEGOSAUR**

ARX ORANO,
FIRST OFFICER

GIPSY SAURINE,
COMMUNICATIONS
OFFICER

IGGY TOOTH,
CHIEF ENGINEER

Jurassic Quadrant

Ankylos

Steggos

Diplox

INDEPENDENT
DINOSAUR
ALLIANCE

vegetarian
sector

Squawk
Major

DSS
UNION OF   PTEROSAURIA
PLANETS

Tri System   Corytho   Lambeos

Iguanos   Aqua Minor

Geldos Cluster

Teerex
Major

Olympus

TYRANNOSAUR
TERRITORIES

carnivore
sector

Planet Sixty

Raptos

THEROPOD EMPIRE

Megalos

Cryptos

vegmeat
zone

(neutral space)

SEA REPTILE
SPACE

Pliosaur
Nurseries

Not to scale

Astrosaurs

THE HATCHING HORROR

by
Steve Cole

Illustrated by
Charlie Fowkes

For Cassie and Nathan

Chapter One

THE EDGE OF EGG-STINCTION!

In a very big hall full of very big dinosaurs, a very big announcement was about to be made.

The Hall of Learning on the planet Odo Minor had never been more packed. Doctors, professors, scientists, TV cameras – they were all squashed up together. The sound of excited dinosaur chatter filled the hall. What was the big news? What had the great Professor Sog discovered now?

But two people in the hall already knew. And one of them didn't seem to care very much.

"I don't see why we had to come all this way!" grumbled Captain Teggs Stegosaur. "I haven't been in a learning hall since I passed my astrosaur exams!"

"Be patient, Captain," his companion Gipsy hissed. "As soon as the talk's over, our mission can begin!"

"About time too," Teggs declared. He was a captain in the Dinosaur Space Service, and he lived for adventure. With his brave crew of astrosaurs, he travelled through space in the DSS *Sauropod*, the finest ship in the Jurassic Quadrant.

Gipsy, a stripy hadrosaur, was his communications officer. She and Teggs had come here to escort Professor Sog back to the *Sauropod* – along with some very special guests . . .

She knew her crewmates would be busy up in orbit. Arx Orano, Teggs's brainy triceratops first officer, would be checking over the *Sauropod*'s systems. And Iggy Tooth, the tough iguanodon engineer, would be stoking the ship's mighty engines.

Their latest voyage into outer space would be their longest yet . . .

"At last," cheered Teggs, making Gipsy jump. "Here comes Professor Sog now!"

Sog was a small, twittery old creature who belonged to a breed called compsognathus. The audience hooted and stamped their feet politely as the funny little figure walked onto the stage. He stopped beside a mysterious, lumpy bundle hidden beneath a black blanket.

A great hush fell on the hall. The dinosaurs waited breathlessly for the professor's words.

Sog struggled to put on a small pair of spectacles. He had trouble reaching his head since his arms were so short. But finally he managed it, and he peered round at the curious crowd.

"Welcome, my friends," he cried. "You are about to hear of a most exciting discovery!"

A bright light started glowing above his head. Seconds later, a hologram of a large, long-necked dinosaur appeared. It looked a bit like a stegosaurus but with a longer neck and tail, and no spiky plates running down its back.

"This is a plateosaurus," said Sog. "Sweet, peaceful – and almost totally extinct."

"Extinct?" asked a puzzled journalist in the crowd.

Sog nodded sadly. "Their race has almost completely died out."

"Dined out?" asked Teggs, perking up. He was famous for his large appetite – some said it was the largest in the whole Dinosaur Space Service. "Dined out where? Can we come too?"

"Not dined out, *died* out!" groaned Gipsy.

Professor Sog continued his talk. "As you all know, we dinosaurs left the Earth long ago. We escaped in spaceships before the meteor struck, never to return. In those days there were many plateosaurus. Nowadays there are hardly any left."

"Why?" someone called.

"Homesickness," said Sog simply. "At

first, they settled on a fine planet called
Platus. But they didn't like it as much as
Earth, so they tried to return." He shook
his head sadly. "Their space fleet flew
into a cosmic storm. Many of their ships
were destroyed.
The few survivors
limped back to
Platus . . . to find
that T. rexes had
taken over."

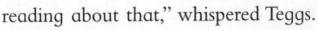

The audience
murmured their
disapproval.

"I remember
reading about that," whispered Teggs.
"The T. rexes wouldn't budge. There was
a big battle."

Gipsy nodded sadly. "And the
plateosaurus lost."

"Other vegetarian races came to
their aid," the professor went on. "As
you know, they joined together and

formed the Dinosaur Space Service, to protect all plant-eaters. In the end they kicked the T. rexes off Platus. But the little planet had been almost ruined by war."

The hologram switched off above Sog's head. "The plateosaurus race never recovered from the tragedy. Today, only a tiny handful survive." He shuffled closer to the black bundle beside him. "But now I bring new hope!"

He clamped his jaws down on the blanket and whipped it away. Beneath it was a pile of eight or nine large white eggs. The audience burst out in gasps and hoots. Flying reptiles flapped nearer with their

TV cameras to get a closer look.

"Plateosaurus eggs!" cried the little professor. "Discovered in a wrecked spaceship far out in the Jurassic Quadrant. That ship was a victim of the cosmic storm. It has drifted through space for thousands of years. But the eggs survived – frozen in space!"

The great hall filled with excited mutterings.

Professor Sog held up his feeble arms for quiet. "As you know, when it comes to hatching I am something of an expert . . ."

"*Eggs*-pert, more like!" Teggs chuckled.

"I was asked to study these old, old eggs," said Sog proudly. "And now that the eggs have thawed out, I believe that they will soon hatch! The plateosaurus race *will* live on!"

The audience cheered, and stamped their feet so hard that the floor shook.

"That's where we come in!" cried Teggs, rising to his feet. He flexed his long, bony tail, and knocked two elderly triceratops off their stools. "Oops!"

Sog frowned at the commotion. "Is that Captain Teggs?"

"Speaking!" he called cheerily, as Gipsy helped up the doddery dinosaurs. "Hello, everyone. It's my mission to take the professor, the eggs, and two plateosaurus guardians to a far-off world called Platus Two. A place where their race can make a fresh start!"

"Is that a fact?!"

Suddenly, the enormous wooden doors at the front of the hall were kicked open. The great hall rang with gasps of shock from the startled crowd.

Teggs narrowed his eyes. In the
doorway stood a dozen small, ugly
creatures. Their short, turtle-like heads
bobbed about on scrawny necks.

One of the creatures darted towards
the stage. "A fresh start for these lovely
little hatchlings?" He shoved Professor
Sog aside. "I don't think so! Not now
the oviraptors are here!"

"Oviraptors?" frowned Teggs.

"Uh-oh!" Gipsy turned to Teggs in
alarm. "They're nest-raiders! Egg-
stealers!"

"We've got to stop them!" yelled Teggs. But he was blocked in on all sides by shocked old dinosaurs.

"I am Prince Goopo, and these are my royal brothers!" The oviraptor snatched up a plateosaurus egg and caressed it with his long, bony fingers. "Eggs are our favourite food, and eggs as rare as *these* will make a meal fit for a king – *and* his princes!" He threw back his head and laughed. "Forget your mission, Captain Teggs. The only place these eggs are going is *into our bellies*!"

Chapter Two

THE EGG-SNATCHERS

"Grub's up, lads!" yelled Prince Goopo.

The oviraptors raced into the learning hall. They moved like lightning. In a second they had stolen every last egg. Then they charged back out through the double doors.

"No!" yelled Teggs. "Get out of my way! They mustn't take the eggs!" He started pushing his way through the dinosaur audience. "You, near the front – stop them!"

But no one took any notice. They were rooted to the ground with shock at what they had just seen.

"Captain, wait!" called Gipsy.

"Catch me up, Gipsy!" Teggs had made it through the crowd, and now he was tearing down the gangway after the egg-snatchers.

With a crash, he burst out of the learning hall and into the beautiful, snowy gardens. He shivered. Winter on Odo Minor was long and cold, and Teggs wished he'd worn his battle armour over his uniform to keep out the chill.

The learning hall was built on a high hilltop with a terrific view. One glance at the churned-up snow at his feet told Teggs where the speedy oviraptors had gone – straight down the hillside.

He charged off after them. Then a small oviraptor popped out from behind a tree – with a laser gun!

Zzzapp! A white-hot laser beam shot over Teggs's head.

"Thanks for warming me up!" Teggs called as he dived for the cover of a nearby bush.

"Just stay where you are, please!" said the oviraptor. He didn't sound as fierce as his brother on the stage. "I hate guns, and I'm a lousy shot."

Teggs frowned. "So why don't you just put down the gun and let me come out?"

"I'd love to," sighed the oviraptor. "But I can't. Goopo would throw a fit. He told me to stop anyone following us while he fetches the ship."

Teggs chewed some frozen leaves for extra strength. "Do you always do what your brother tells you?" he asked, creeping quietly closer.

"Goopo's the eldest. He'll be king someday." The little figure sighed. "I'm Prince Shelly, the youngest – so I never get any say in what goes on. Now, stay back! I don't want to hurt you!"

"That makes two of us!" called Teggs. Slowly, his big bony tail snaked out from the undergrowth and curled itself around Prince Shelly . . .

"Got you!" Teggs cried.

The oviraptor gasped as Teggs's tail tightened round him – he was trapped!

Teggs dragged his prisoner over to the top of the steep hillside. Goopo and his brothers were nearing the bottom of the slope. Soon they would vanish into the woods, and Teggs would never find them.

He dangled Shelly over the edge of the hillside. "You know, I think it's time you caught up with your brothers," he grinned. "There's *snow* time to lose!"

With that, Teggs flung Shelly down the hillside after his brothers. The raptor hit the snow with a yelp. Unable to stop himself, he rolled over and over. And as he rolled, he gathered snow – faster and faster. Soon, he looked like a giant squawking snowball. As he tumbled towards the fleeing oviraptors he got bigger and rounder and heavier . . .

Until finally – *Splat!* The snowball rolled right over Goopo and his brothers, squashing them into the snow.

"Direct hit!" cheered Teggs. Then he sledged down the hill on his tummy to round up the oviraptors and recover the eggs. Luckily, the soft snow had stopped them from breaking – and the oviraptors were unharmed too.

Up close, they were not pretty creatures. Their jaws were wide and toothless – instead, they used two bony prongs inside their mouths to crack open their food. Each of the creatures had a high, narrow crest rising up from its head.

Teggs smiled at the dazed reptiles. "That should cool you off till the space police arrive!"

"Curse you, Captain!" snarled Prince Goopo, half-buried by snow. "I command you to release us in the name of our king!"

"No way," said Teggs. "Anyway, I'm sure your king would be very cross if he knew you were stealing such important eggs!"

"Pah!" cried Goopo. "It was his idea! King Albu will kill us if we don't bring him those eggs!"

"He'll fry us with butter!" twittered another oviraptor.

"He'll boil us in salty water for three minutes!" moaned a third.

"And then he'll crack our heads with a big spoon!" quaked one more.

"It's quite exhausting," sighed Prince Shelly, still stuck in his giant snowball. "Me and my brothers are sent out round the universe in search of tasty new treats for the royal menu. Goopo's right. If we fail . . .

the king will have us served with toast soldiers!"

Just then, Gipsy came scampering down the hill. "There you are, Captain!" she beamed as she reached the bottom. "I see you've caught the thieves!"

Teggs winked at her. "Better still, the eggs are safe and sound!"

Gipsy frowned. "But, Captain—"

Whatever Gipsy said, Teggs didn't hear it. For with a mighty roar of engines, a strange spaceship rose up into the sky above the forest. It was a long, narrow rocket with two spinning engines at one end, like an enormous egg-whisk.

Goopo laughed. "Using Shelly to squash us was a good trick, Captain," he said. "But Prince Hibbit was too quick for you! He got away to the woods and fetched the ship!"

Teggs and Gipsy backed away as the spaceship came in to land. Prince Hibbit was leaning out of the window, pulling rude faces. The heat from the ship's whisking engines soon melted the nearby snow, and his brothers shook themselves free.

Hibbit fired a laser bolt at Teggs. It missed by millimetres. He and Gipsy were forced back.

"Get on board, brothers!" Goopo cried. "We won't be cracked, scrambled, and mixed with mayonnaise *this* day!"

In the wink of an eye, the soggy oviraptors had bundled back on board with the stolen eggs. Shelly was the last inside. With a sad little wave at Teggs and Gipsy, he vanished into the ship. It took off at once.

Teggs spoke into the communicator strapped to his arm. "Teggs to *Sauropod*! Arx, can you hear me? An oviraptor ship is getting away! Stop them!" He looked helplessly at Gipsy. "I don't believe it! I've let them take the eggs – I've failed!"

Chapter Three

EXPECT THE UN-EGGS-PECTED!

On the flight deck of the DSS *Sauropod*, high above the planet, Arx Orano heard his captain's cry.

"Quick!" the triceratops barked at his flight crew. "Switch on the scanners! Find that spaceship!"

The flight crew were dimorphodon, highly trained flying reptiles. They clucked and flapped about the dinosaur

spaceship, pulling levers and flicking switches.

The scanner soon showed the oviraptor ship soaring away at top speed.

"Fire lasers!" Arx ordered.

Beams of light fired from the *Sauropod*. But the oviraptor ship quickly whisked away out of range. Not a single shot found its mark.

Arx sighed and nudged the communicator with his nose horn. "Captain? This is Arx. I'm afraid the oviraptors were too quick for us. They've got away!"

★

Captain Teggs felt awful as he walked back to the Hall of Learning. His head hung down in shame. Gipsy patted him on the side of his neck with a gentle hoof. "It's all right, Captain," she said. "There's nothing to worry about!"

"Oh yeah?" Teggs waved his spiky tail towards the crowds that were starting to spill out from the hall. "Let's see if *they* agree with you!"

Professor Sog was leading his fellow dinosaurs outside. The perky little reptile was hopping about with excitement.

"Well done, Captain!" he chirped. "Your concern was very convincing. Those 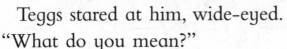 oviraptors are bound to think they've stolen the *real* eggs!"

Teggs stared at him, wide-eyed. "What do you mean?"

"Those eggs on the stage were fakes!" Sog chuckled. "They were just props! I brought them along to spice up my talk."

Teggs whooped with relief. "Then where *are* the real eggs?"

"Here!" came a low, lazy voice from the crowd. Two large, long-necked creatures stomped into view. Teggs recognized them from the professor's hologram – they were plateosaurus. They each carried a large shiny box around their necks.

"I am Coo," said one of the
dinosaurs.

"And I am Dippa," said the other, a
female. "We are the guardians of the
eggs."

Coo bobbed his head at the box
round Dippa's neck. "I watch her eggs."

"And I watch his," Dippa explained.

"So now the mission can begin!"
Professor Sog was still merrily leaping
about. "Oh, I'd love to see King Albu's
face when he tries to eat those eggs!"

Way out in space, at the sticky centre of his royal ship, King Albu sat waiting on his golden throne. Thick drool bubbled out of his mouth and stained his royal robes at the thought of his next meal – fried plateosaurus eggs on toast!

King Albu waited.

And waited.

His tummy rumbled loud enough to make the walls shake. And *still* he waited.

At last, King Albu could bear it no more. He turned to the nearest slave and shouted: "Fetch me Prince Goopo – now!"

The slave rushed from the room. Less than a minute later, Prince Goopo came in. He looked very worried.

"Where are my eggs?" hissed King Albu.

Prince Goopo gulped. "I think . . . er . . . I think Cook was having a little trouble bringing out their full flavour . . ."

"Fetch me the cook at once!" screamed King Albu.

Prince Goopo crawled out of the room at top speed. In seconds, he had returned with the cook, who looked red-faced and nervous.

"Where's my supper?" roared the king.

"Erm . . ." The cook crossed his legs like he needed the toilet. "They are . . . er . . . very tough to cook."

"So?" growled King Albu. "Just serve 'em up as they are!"

"Forgive me, Your

Egginess," said the cook. "But I really don't think—"

"Look, Cook. I like 'em soft. I like 'em hard. I like sucking out the yolk with a straw. I like paddling in the egg whites then licking my feet clean."

The slaves nodded solemnly. They had seen him do such things lots of times.

"I like 'em raw. I like 'em fried. I like 'em thin. I like 'em wide." King Albu narrowed his eyes and widened his mouth. "In short, *I like my eggs*, Cook! And I want a piled-up plate of plateosaurus eggs right now!"

The cook sighed and went outside. He returned with a silver trolley piled high with a grassy salad – and several giant eggs.

"At last!" drooled the king. He grasped an egg in both hands. Then he opened his mouth as wide as it would go, and popped it inside.

Where it stuck!

The egg could not be crushed or chewed or slurped down or guzzled. It stuck right in his throat. King Albu's scaly neck looked like a snake that had swallowed a rugby ball!

"Urph!" he choked. "That's not an egg! It's a *rock*! A painted rock!" He ran around, clutching the large lump in his neck. "You idiot, Goopo! I send you out for eggs and you bring back *boulders*!"

With a strangled yell, King Albu choked up the enormous fake egg and kicked it across the room.

"My stomach wants plateosaurus eggs!" he panted. "And my stomach will not take no for an answer! Get your brothers together, Goopo. We're going to get our hands on those eggs – whatever it takes!"

Chapter Four

THE LONG, LONG JOURNEY

Back on Odo Minor, Iggy the engineer was waiting for his captain in the *Sauropod*'s shuttle. When Teggs poked his head through the door, the iguanodon saluted stiffly.

"Ready for boarding, Captain!" he cried.

"It's going to be a tight squeeze,
Iggy!" grinned Teggs. He came aboard,
with Gipsy close behind. Then Coo and
Dippa squeezed in through the shuttle's
doorway. They shuffled close together
and Professor Sog hopped aboard
beside them.

"I still can't believe the oviraptors
went to all that trouble just to steal a
lot of painted rocks!" laughed Teggs.
"That'll give King Albu an upset
tummy!"

"It sure will," laughed Gipsy, as the shuttle blasted off into space. "And meanwhile, we'll make sure the *real* eggs reach Platus Two – safe and sound and ready for hatching!"

Soon the *Sauropod* was racing through space.

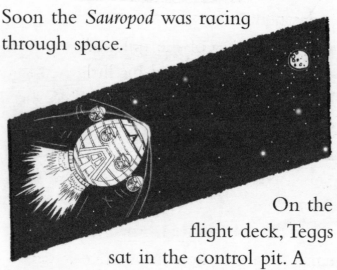

On the flight deck, Teggs sat in the control pit. A feeling of excitement was building in his belly. His mission had begun. And with the eggs almost ready to hatch, there was no time to lose!

Arx turned on the scanner. Tiny stars gleamed in the darkness of space. "That's where we're headed," he said.

"The very edge of the galaxy."

Professor Sog nodded his little head. "I'm looking forward to seeing Platus Two!"

Gipsy wrinkled her snout, puzzled. "You mean you haven't been there before?"

"No one's been there for hundreds of years," Sog told her. "Not since it was first discovered by the Jurassic Explorers."

"Wow," breathed Teggs. The Jurassic Explorers were his heroes. They were the reason he had become an astrosaur. Long before he was born, they had discovered and mapped the entire

Jurassic Quadrant, where all dinosaurs now lived. The only thing they had never found was a star dragon – a huge, winged animal that was said to live somewhere in space. It was Teggs's dream that maybe one day he would find a star dragon himself.

"Why has no one ever gone to live on Platus Two?" asked Gipsy.

"It's too small and far away from everywhere else," said Sog.

"So we'll be the first spaceship to go there in centuries!" Teggs realized.

Arx nodded. "I wonder what it's like?"

"It'll be lovely, just you wait and see!" smiled Sog. "The explorers planted lots of seeds there. After hundreds of years it should be very green indeed!" He chuckled. "Yes, Platus Two may be too far away to matter to most dinosaurs. But it's the perfect spot for a small herd of peaceful plateosaurus!"

"Hope so," sighed Coo. "A new home would be nice, wouldn't it, Dippa?"

"It would, Coo," Dippa agreed.

Just then the ship shook with a sudden *clunk!* The dimorphodon flight crew squawked and then flapped in panic about the room.

"Battle stations!" cried Teggs.

Arx squinted at his instruments. "No sign of hostile ships," he reported. "Only a meteor, bouncing off the side of the ship."

"Oh," said Teggs, a tiny bit disappointed.

"Funny," said Arx. "It seems to be following us."

"It must have got caught in our gravity field," said Professor Sog.

"I suppose so," Arx nodded. "But I've never known a meteor do that before."

"We're out in deep space now," said Gipsy. She looked a bit spooked. "Who knows what we'll find out here?"

"We'll find Platus Two, that's what!" said Sog firmly. "Don't let your imagination run away with you, child!"

But as the *Sauropod* sped on to its destination, Gipsy found it was hard not to.

Days passed by and the stars grew fewer and fainter.

Space grew blacker and blacker.

And Captain Teggs began to grow bored. For the first few days he'd kept a careful watch for star dragons. But he could find no sign of one anywhere.

By the end of the first week, the scanner was showing nothing but blackness. The *Sauropod* was like a big fish swimming through the darkest sea in the universe.

"Hey, that's strange," said Arx, looking at a computer screen. "We're *still* dragging along that meteor we bumped into."

"Never mind boring old meteors," said Teggs. "Who's for another game of I-Spy?"

The days dragged on. But at the end of the *second* week, they could at last see Platus Two on the scanners.

And Arx made a strange discovery.

He called everyone to the flight deck to tell them about it.

"Well, Arx?" said Teggs, settling back into the control pit after a long doze.

"I've been studying Platus Two closely, Captain," the triceratops announced. "And something's wrong. I've checked my findings against the notes made by the Jurassic Explorers – and they're completely different!"

Teggs frowned as he chewed some moss. "Different in what way?"

Arx looked at him. "Since the Jurassic Explorers visited Platus Two, it has grown *ten times bigger!*"

"Impossible!" Sog said crossly. He tried to fold his arms but they wouldn't quite reach, which made him even crosser. "Planets do not grow like living things! Arx, you must be wrong! Your instruments are faulty!"

At that, Arx got a bit huffy, and Teggs quickly butted in before a big row started.

"Can you show us Platus Two on the scanners, Arx?" he asked.

Arx jabbed a button with his horn. On the screen, Platus Two glowed bright against black space. Pure white and smooth, it looked like a giant snooker ball.

Then a rocky shape drifted into view.

"It's that stupid meteor again," grumbled Arx.

"But I thought it was trailing behind us," said Teggs. "How come it's now heading *straight for us?*"

A split-second later, Teggs got his answer. Everyone jumped as the meteor suddenly split right open! Bursting from inside it – like a terrifying creature hatching from a giant egg – was a familiar whisk-like ship.

"Oviraptors!" gasped Gipsy.

Arx nodded grimly. "They disguised their ship as a meteor and tagged along all the way here!"

"They want our eggs!" wailed Coo.

"Oh dear," said Dippa.

Suddenly the oviraptor ship fired its lasers. Two balls of flame streaked towards them.

"Red alert!" shouted Teggs. "We're under attack!"

Chapter Five

LIGHTNING STRIKES TWICE

Twin bolts of fire slammed into the *Sauropod*. The ship shook like a jelly in an earthquake. Then it tipped up. Coo and Dippa screamed, their egg boxes clanging together like giant bells. Professor Sog was sent somersaulting up to the ceiling. The dimorphodon flight crew screeched and flapped into each other.

Teggs fought to keep his balance in the control pit. Flapping reptiles collided above him. The squawk of the alarm pterosaur echoed round the ship: "*Red alert! Red alert!*"

"Damage report!" cried Teggs.

Iggy came tumbling out of the lift and onto the flight deck. "Message from the engine room, Captain!" he yelled. "Engines have been hit!"

"We can't get away now!" cried Sog, as a pair of flying reptiles helped him down from the ceiling.

"Fire lasers," snapped Teggs.

"Lasers have jammed!" Gipsy reported.

"All right then, fire the dung torpedoes!" he ordered.

Gipsy flicked a row of switches with her tail. "Firing now!"

On the scanner, a brown explosion lit up the oviraptor ship. "Direct hit!" cheered Arx.

"That should cause a stink on the oviraptor ship!" grinned Iggy.

"Message coming in," Gipsy reported. "It's King Albu!"

"Put him on screen," Teggs said.

Everyone watched as an ugly, stubby little creature appeared on the screen. He wore a large crown on his head and an even larger clothes peg on his snout.

Teggs smiled grimly. "I see that you've felt – and smelled – what our dung torpedoes can do, King Albu. Leave now, and we'll say no more about it."

King Albu shook his head. "Doo hab dum-fing I vant, Dap-tin," he hissed.

"Er . . . pardon?" asked Teggs.

The royal oviraptor pulled the peg from his nose. "I said, you have something I want, Captain!"

"You really came all this way just to eat the plateosaurus eggs?" Teggs shook his head sadly. "You have to be crazy!"

"I certainly am," King Albu agreed. "So hand them over – or else my power poachers will turn you into toast!"

Teggs shook his head. "Try that and the next round of dung torpedoes will knock your noses clean off!"

"I don't think so, Captain." King Albu smiled nastily. "Your engines run on dung, and we've just blasted them open. You can't afford to waste any more fuel."

Iggy sighed. "He's right, Captain!"

"Oh well," sighed Coo. "I suppose we'd better let him have the eggs, then."

"Yes, that's probably best," agreed Dippa. "Never mind."

"Never mind?" Teggs stared at them. "This is the future of your people we're talking about!"

"But there's nothing we can do," said Coo.

"There's always *something* we can do," said Teggs bravely.

"Like what?" asked Professor Sog.

Everyone looked at Teggs.

"Well . . . we need to repair our engines. And for that, we need to land." He nodded firmly. "We must head for Platus Two. Now!"

"But we can't outrun King Albu, Captain!" said Iggy.

"We have to try!" Teggs snapped.

"We might just lose them in the clouds. Maybe we'll buy enough time to fix the damage."

"It's a brave plan, Captain," said Arx with a small smile.

Gipsy clapped her claws together and called to the flight crew. "Let's do it, team!"

The *Sauropod*'s engines hummed weakly. With a lurch, they were off.

"Don't say I didn't warn you, Captain!" snarled King Albu. He put the clothes peg back on his nose and turned to his crew. "Dopen vire!" he shouted.

"Eh?" Teggs frowned.

An ear-splitting explosion ripped through the *Sauropod*. The whole ship shook even harder than before.

"He said, 'Open fire'," said Arx helpfully.

"Approaching Platus Two," said Gipsy. "Entering clouds now."

"Take that oviraptor off the screen!" said Teggs. "Let's have a look!"

King Albu's evil face was replaced by a close-up view of the cloudy white planet.

"Take us in low," Teggs ordered. "We'll try to steer round behind him and stay out of sight."

"Such a shame," sighed Sog. "We're already fighting over this calm and peaceful world."

"Er . . . calm and peaceful, you say?"

echoed Teggs, looking at the screen.

They had broken through the clouds. Now they could see what the planet was really like.

It was horrible.

The pale ground was smooth and speckled, but criss-crossed with huge cracks as if it was ready to fall apart. There were no hills or trees, no flowers or animals. Everywhere was flat and featureless, and a fierce storm was raging overhead. Lightning hurled bright daggers down at the ground. Great fountains of sticky lava spurted up to the clouds in revenge.

Dippa sighed. "Not very green, is it?"

"But – but this is terrible!" squawked Professor Sog. "The explorers planted seeds! Why haven't they grown?"

"*Now* will you believe me?" said Arx. "This can't be Platus Two at all. It's a different world!"

"No!" Sog insisted. "I checked the

star charts! This is right where Platus Two should be!"

Coo and Dippa just stared sadly at the screen.

"Captain!" shouted Gipsy. "The oviraptors have found us! Look!"

King Albu's ship was swooping out of the clouds towards them.

"We have to go faster!" Teggs cried.

"We can't!" yelled Iggy.

Then, just as everything seemed hopeless, a jagged blast of yellow light struck the oviraptor ship — and it fell from the sky like a stone.

"Lightning!" beamed Teggs. "King Albu's ship has been struck by lightning!"

"Serves them right," said Iggy.

"We're saved!" Professor Sog did a little victory jig. "Yippee!"

But suddenly, the scanner glowed white-hot. A crisp crackling noise rasped through the air. Sparks flew round the flight deck. Sog stopped dancing, and the dimorphodon flapped round in panic.

"Ooops," said Arx. "Now *we've* been struck by lightning!"

The engines spluttered and died.

"We're going down!" shouted Iggy.

"Attention, crew!" Teggs yelled. "Brace yourselves! We're going to crash!"

"We're going to crash!" squawked the alarm pterosaur. "*We're going to crash!*"

On the scanner, the ground came rushing up to meet them . . .

Chapter Six

THE MYSTERIOUS PLANET

Ka-boom!

Tumbling out of control, the *Sauropod* scraped against the smooth surface of the planet.

B-B-B-B-B-B-B-B-B-Bang!

The ship flipped up and over. It splattered through one of the red-hot geysers spurting out of the ground.

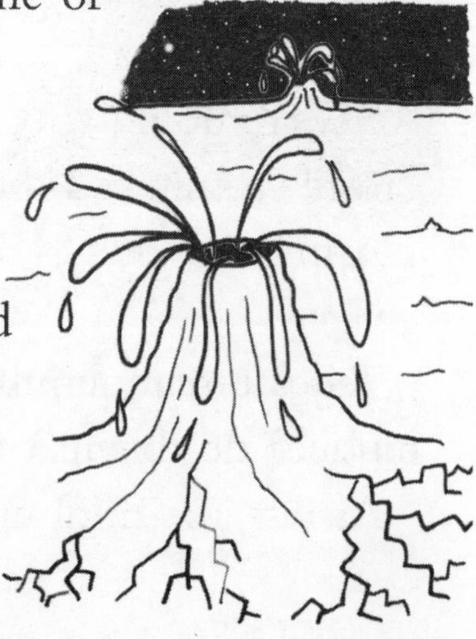

"She can't take much more!" howled Iggy.

"Neither can we!" gasped Dippa.

A long, wide crack had opened up
beneath them. The *Sauropod* fell through
the crack and started bouncing
between the sides. Then a fresh spurt of
sticky lava pushed them high up into
the air.

Teggs braced himself. "What goes up,
must come down!"
At last, the final crash came.

No one on board the *Sauropod* had ever heard a noise like it.

It was a crumpling, rumpling, bone-crushing, head-mushing, grinding, gruelling, wrenching, bottom-clenching *smash*.

Then the ship was still.

Slowly, Coo raised his long, aching neck. "I wish I'd stayed at home," he sighed.

"Now we know how the meteor felt when it smashed into the Earth," groaned Teggs.

Professor Sog peered out from under a chair. "The eggs!" he twittered. "Dippa, Coo – what about the eggs?"

The two plateosaurus checked their egg boxes.

"Unscrambled," Dippa reported.

"Wish I could say the same for my brains," said Teggs.

Iggy waddled over to the communicator. "Calling engine room, this is Iggy. Are you all right, boys?"

Assorted moans and groans came from the speaker.

"Just about!" someone said.

"Good," said Teggs. "Everyone's OK. But remember, if *we* made it through the landing, chances are that King Albu and his egg-snatchers did too." He hungrily uprooted an enormous fern and swallowed it down. "And there's nothing like a really big crash for working up an appetite!"

"Perhaps we should *all* get eating," said Arx gravely. "We need to make more fuel for the engines."

"Of course," said Gipsy, wrinkling her nose. "More dung!"

"It's a big job," said Teggs. "*Several* big jobs, in fact."

"Leave it to me and my boys," smiled Iggy. "We'll have a good meal while we fix the engines. Then we'll fill them up for you – no sweat!"

Teggs saluted him. "I knew I could count on you!"

Iggy saluted in return, and left the flight deck.

Gipsy pulled a face. "Well, while Iggy gets to the *bottom* of things in the engine room, I'll try to listen in on the oviraptors."

"Good idea," said Teggs. "We might learn what they're planning."

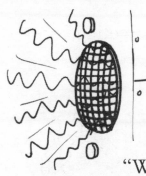

Gipsy's hands flicked over the controls. Suddenly, a spooky wailing sound crackled out of the speakers.

"What is *that*?" asked Teggs.

"Sounds like a ghost!" said Dippa.

"Or faulty speakers," Arx added.

"I think it sounded like someone in distress," said Gipsy. She pressed some more buttons. "Yes, I've got a fix on the signal now. It's coming from somewhere outside!"

"Impossible!" snapped Professor Sog. "How could anyone live in this terrible place?"

"We'd better find out," said Teggs. "Because if we can't get the ship fixed – we'll be joining them!"

The crew got ready to go outside. Then they gathered at the ship's main hatchway.

Teggs had changed into his battle
armour, and Gipsy had slipped on her
combat suit. If it came to a fight, they
would be ready.

Gipsy joined Teggs as he stared out
onto the strange, dark planet.

"Do you think we'll really get out of
this mess?" she whispered.

"We've got to, Gipsy," said Teggs
softly. He gave her a crooked smile. "I
can't stop exploring space yet! I haven't
discovered my very own star dragon!"

"Speaking of discoveries . . ." said Arx, shuffling over. "I wonder what we'll find out there?"

"Well, whoever was making that noise, we can find them with this," said Gipsy, tapping a gadget on her wrist. "It's a special tracker. The faster it bleeps, the closer we are."

"Why can't we just hide on the *Sauropod* until Iggy's fixed the engines?" asked Dippa.

Teggs shook his head. "If the oviraptors come aboard, they'll sniff out the eggs in seconds. Out there in the storm, they'll find it harder. Besides, Iggy and the boys have some important jobs to do. They mustn't be put off by a load of rotten reptiles running about."

Just then, a flash of lightning lit up

the sky. Gipsy thought she caught a glimpse of something moving just outside.

"We'd better get going," she said nervously.

Teggs led the way out onto the surface of the unpleasant planet, through the howling wind and the drenching rain. The ground was smooth and slippery beneath their feet. He had the feeling they were being watched.

Lightning flashed again. Teggs caught a sudden movement from the corner of his eye. Dark shapes, small and nasty, creeping towards them.

"Look out!" he yelled. "It's the oviraptors!"

"It sure is," gurgled Goopo.

"Worst luck for you!" snarled King Albu.

He snapped his claws

and his sons rushed to form a tight
circle around the dinosaurs. Teggs saw
now that each of them held a ray gun.

"We're trapped!" gasped Gipsy.

Arx lowered his horns. "I could
charge them, Captain."

"They'd blast you before you got
close," hissed Teggs. "I won't let them
add roast triceratops to their mad
menu!"

"Now then, Captain Teggs," said King Albu. "You know what I want: eggs!" A dreamy look came into his eyes. "Yes, I said eggs! E-G-G-S. Eggs, eggs, eggs, eggs." He started drooling. "Eggggggggggggggs, mmmmmm."

One by one, his sons started dribbling too. "Eggggggggs," they echoed.

But not Prince Shelly. He threw down his gun crossly. "This is *silly*, Father!" he complained. "Our ship's lying in pieces! We're stranded billions of miles from home! And all you care about are a few lousy eggs!"

"Lousy?" gasped King Albu in shock. "You dare . . . to call eggs . . . *lousy*?"

The oviraptors all booed and hissed Prince Shelly.

And while they were distracted, Teggs struck.

He lashed out with his armoured tail. Blue sparks shot from the end, and four of the little reptiles were sent flying.

"Now, Arx!" Teggs cried.

The triceratops charged at Prince Goopo, who cried out in terror and ran. He screeched so loudly that the others dropped their guns as they scrabbled to block their ears.

Then Gipsy sprang into action. With

a few well-placed jabs, kicks and tail-swipes she flattened five more of the oviraptors.

But King Albu had grabbed one of the ray guns. He started firing wildly. Bolts of white light sizzled through the air.

"Run!" cried Teggs as one of the laser beams whistled past his ear.

Rushing for cover, Arx and Coo went one way while Gipsy and Sog went another. Dippa ran off all by herself, so

Teggs chased after her.

"Just you wait, acorn-brain!" roared King Albu. "I'll get those eggs yet!"

"Not if I can help it," muttered Teggs. He swung his head about wildly, looking for somewhere to hide from the gunfire. But the landscape was smooth and flat on all sides.

"Look out!" called Dippa.

Teggs skidded to a stop just in front of a huge gash in the ground. It was too wide to jump over.

"We'll have to turn back!" wailed Dippa.

"We can't!" said Teggs. As if to prove it, a laser beam whizzed past between them. "There's only one place we can go now!"

Teggs was pointing to the crack in the ground. "Down *there*?" Dippa gulped.

"Now!" cried Teggs.

Together, the two dinosaurs leaped into the blackness.

Chapter Seven

THE TUNNELS OF FEAR

Luckily, Teggs and Dippa didn't have far to fall. They landed with a thump on a small ledge.

"Did you know this was here?" gasped Dippa.

"Er . . . of course!" said Teggs quickly.

Dippa peered over the edge. "How deep is this crack?" she wondered. "And what's at the bottom of it?"

A spooky, wailing noise rose up from the darkness. It was the same noise they had heard back on the *Sauropod*.

"Who needs Gipsy's tracker?" said Teggs. "Whatever that thing is, it's right beneath us!" He explored along the ledge a little further. Soon the winking lights on his battle helmet lit up a jagged gash in the smooth rock beside him. "It's another crack . . . a sort of passageway! Come on, before the oviraptors find us."

"I don't like scary passageways," whispered Dippa. "Why don't we just let King Albu *have* the eggs?"

Teggs stared at her. "How can you even think such a thing?"

Dippa shrugged. "It would be much easier."

"It would be easier, but it would be *wrong*," said Teggs sternly. "Those eggs hold the future of your race! Isn't that worth fighting for?"

"Fighting ruined our old world," said Dippa. "Fighting is bad."

"But giving up is bad too, Dippa," Teggs told her. "I know you're scared. I am too! But you mustn't throw away your dreams."

Dippa nodded slowly. "I dream of a new place to call home," she said. "I dream of having little baby plateosaurus to look after. I dream that one day there will be a whole, happy herd of us on our own planet."

"Then *fight* for those dreams," Teggs told her.

Just then, they heard a scuttling sound above them. "This way, boys!" came a familiar, wicked voice. "There's a ledge! They must have jumped down here!"

"King Albu!" hissed Teggs. "Quick!
Let's get going!"

He and Dippa started galloping
through the darkness on all fours. The
oviraptors soon figured out where they
had gone, and gave chase.

"They're catching up!" panted Dippa.

"Keep running!" cried Teggs.

Then the mysterious, ghostly wail
started up again, chilling them to the
bone. Teggs and Dippa skidded to a
halt, and so did the oviraptor princes.
Teggs saw them by the light of his

battle helmet, clutching each other in fear.

"We – we *have* to go back now, Father!" stammered Shelly.

"Never!" cried King Albu. "Now, grab those eggs, boys – or I'll hard-boil you all!"

Goopo and his brothers slowly advanced on the two herbivores.

"Get behind me, Dippa," hissed Teggs. "Maybe I can scare them off." He flexed his armoured tail, ready to fight. But the passage was too small, and his tail was too big. It whacked against the smooth wall and suddenly, the whole passageway started to shake.

"Look out, Dippa!" shouted Teggs. "The walls are caving in!"

"Eeek!" squeaked Goopo. He turned and fled, his brothers close behind. Teggs and Dippa huddled together as big speckled slabs kept on falling. Soon the passage was completely blocked. They were safe from the oviraptors – but now there was no way back to the *Sauropod*.

"There's only one path we can take now," said Teggs quietly. "But it'll lead us right to whatever's been making that terrible noise!"

Meanwhile, Gipsy and Sog were huddled outside in a howling gale, wishing they were warm and safe back on the *Sauropod*. Like Teggs and Dippa, they had hidden in one of the great splits in the planet's surface. But the ledge they were creeping along was very narrow. One slip, and they would fall to their doom.

"I wonder what caused all these cracks," said Sog nervously. "If it was an earthquake, where's all the rubble? There's not a single loose stone round here!"

"Maybe it's special, super-tough rock," said Gipsy. "That's why the explorers' seeds never grew." Gipsy's tracker started beeping loudly. "You know, this thing is going crazy. It reckons the source of that signal is . . . everywhere!"

"Shhh!" gasped the little professor. "I think something's coming!"

He was right. Something heavy was creeping along the ledge in the opposite direction — straight towards them.

"It's too dark!" hissed Gipsy. "I can't see what it is!"

"It's the thing that made that terrible wailing noise!" cried Sog. "I know it is!"

He hopped onto Gipsy's tail and scampered up to her shoulder in fright.

The footsteps shuffled closer and closer . . .

Chapter Eight

THE SECRET OF PLATUS TWO

"Halt!" squawked Professor Sog bravely. He peered out from behind the crest on Gipsy's head. "Who goes there?"

A familiar figure came out of the shadows. "Hello, Gipsy! Professor!"

"Arx!" squealed Gipsy in delight.

"And me!" called Coo from somewhere behind him.

"Thank goodness!" gasped Sog. "So, you hid in the crack too!"

"There was nowhere else to go," said Arx. He seemed a little out of breath. "I'm glad we've found you. There's something I think you should see."

"What is it?" asked Gipsy.

But Arx was already retracing his footsteps. "The path gets very steep down here. Don't slip!"

Gipsy and Sog followed them along the ledge. Arx was right – the path dipped down sharply. Gipsy trod carefully, while Sog slithered down on his bottom.

The air grew warmer. The ledge grew wider. A soft, thudding noise seemed to echo up from the chasm beside them.

To Gipsy, it sounded like a huge,

heavy heartbeat. Her tracker bleeped so loudly she had to turn it off.

They crept on for what felt like ages. Then, suddenly, the steep path levelled out. Arx came to a sudden stop.

"Here we are," he said. "A hole. I think it stretches down to the very centre of the planet!"

Gipsy stared down into the hole. This was the source of the heartbeat sound: *Ba-DUMP . . . Ba-DUMP . . . Ba-DUMP . . .*

It was like looking into a deep well. Far below, thick yellowy-white liquid sloshed about like runny custard.

"Keep watching," Arx murmured.

Then, just below the slimy surface of the goo . . . something massive moved!

"What was that?" Gipsy gasped.

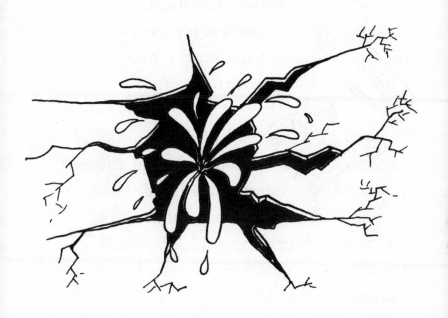

"I think I know," said Arx. "But if I'm right, we're in worse trouble than we thought!"

Even as he spoke, the wall behind them exploded with a mighty crash!

Coo yelped as bits of the strange, smooth rock flew through the air. Sog hid behind Arx's head for safety.

Gipsy whirled around in surprise. "Look!" she cried. A huge hole had

appeared in the smooth wall.
"Something's coming out!"

A familiar orange head poked
out of the darkness.
"Only me!"

"Captain Teggs!"
beamed Gipsy.
She quickly saluted.
"And Dippa! You
gave us a fright!"

"Sorry about that,"
said Teggs. "We were
walking through one of the cracks,
but it came to a dead end."

"So he smashed through the rock
with his tail!" added Dippa.

"Rock, eh?" said Arx. He nudged a
fragment of the smooth rock with his
horn. "I'm not so sure . . . See how
easily this stuff breaks?"

Teggs looked hurt. "Well, I did give it
quite a whack, you know!"

"I'm sure you did, Captain," said Arx

quickly. "But look at it! So smooth, so brittle. It's not really like rock at all, is it?"

Everyone stared at the broken pieces on the ground.

"You're right," said Teggs slowly. "In fact, it looks a lot like . . . *eggshell*!"

"Eggshell?" twittered Sog. "But this material covers the whole planet!"

"I don't get it," said Coo. "How can a planet be made from eggshell?"

"Easy," said Arx. "Because Platus Two *isn't* a planet after all! It's an *egg*! A SPECIAL, GIGANTIC, PLANET-SIZED EGG!"

Everyone stared at him in amazement.

"Of course!" breathed Teggs. "It makes perfect sense!"

"Seems crazy to me," said Dippa.

"Ah, but things aren't always as they seem," said Teggs. "Remember the way the oviraptor ship was hidden inside the meteor? This is the same idea – only there's something a lot bigger hidden inside this planet!"

Arx turned to Professor Sog. "I *told* you Platus Two had grown!" he cried. "It's probably been getting bigger and bigger for hundreds of years – because the creature *inside it* has been growing in size too!"

"But – but eggs don't grow!" protested Sog.

"This is no ordinary egg," said Arx. "Besides, can *you* imagine laying an egg the size of a planet?"

"Ouch!" Teggs winced. "That would

bring tears to your
eyes!"

"So let me get this
straight," said Gipsy
excitedly. "The
explorers mistook
Platus Two for a
planet, just like we did.
But deep inside it is the
biggest baby in the universe – and it's
starting to hatch!"

"That's why there are cracks all over
the place!" said Teggs. "The thick shell
is breaking open!"

"What about those geysers?" asked
Coo. "How can an egg spray molten
lava everywhere?"

"But it's *not* molten lava," Gipsy told
him. "It's just egg white bursting out as
the egg starts to hatch!"

"Well, what about that scary noise?"
asked Dippa.

"Come on," said Arx, like a stern

schoolteacher. "What's the first thing a baby does when it hatches?"

"It cries!" Dippa realized. "That's what we've been hearing!"

They all stared down into the deep, dark hole, where the baby was slowly stirring in its runny yolk.

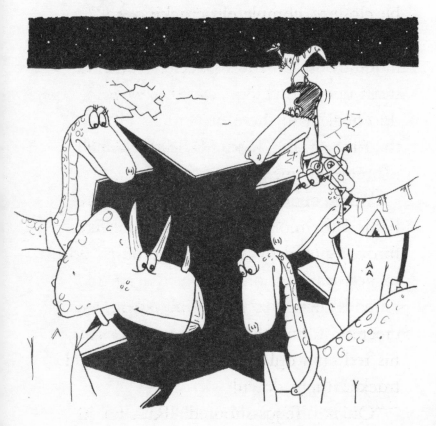

"Think how big it must be,"
whispered Sog. "Simply enormous! That
movement we saw was probably just
an eyelash! Or the tip of a whisker!"

"Uh-oh," said Gipsy. "I just had an
awful thought. If this creature really *is*
ready to hatch, then Platus Two must
be close to completely cracking up!"

"I know how it feels," sighed Coo.

"Guys," said Teggs gravely, "if we
can't get off this egg-world – we're
doomed!"

"You're right!" Sog squealed. "We'll
all be flung off into space!"

"Flung off into space?" said someone
behind them. "Ha! That will seem like
fun compared to what *I'm* going to do
to you all!"

Teggs turned to find King Albu
creeping along the ledge towards them,
his red eyes agleam. The oviraptors had
tracked them down!

"Quick!" Teggs shouted. "Run for it!"

But then Prince Goopo led his brothers out of the shadows, blocking their way.

King Albu giggled with glee. "This time, there will be no escape!"

Chapter Nine

A STICKY END

"Listen, you egg-mad maniac!" shouted Teggs. "This whole world is about to break apart! We have to get out of here – and fast. If we work together, maybe we can—"

"Nope." King Albu shook his head.

"I'm not doing a single thing until I've
eaten those eggs. So *nyah!*"

Coo lumbered forwards. "All right
then," he said. "I suppose you'd better
have them."

"No!" shouted Dippa. "I won't let
you!" She slammed her mighty tail
down on the ground in front of Coo.

Coo froze. Everyone stared at Dippa in amazement – even King Albu.

"Captain Teggs is right," she said. "Those eggs are our future, Coo. And the future is worth fighting for."

"It is?" Coo blinked in surprise. "Oh. Well, if you really think so . . ."

Dippa smiled at Teggs. "I *know* so."

"You know nothing!" spat King Albu. "Come on! Eggs! Now!"

But even as he spoke, the ground started to shake. A fountain of steaming hot goo burst out from the deep dark hole in the ground.

"See that, King Albu?" Teggs yelled. "That's *egg white*. This whole place is bursting with the stuff! Why are you bothering with a few measly plateosaurus eggs?

The biggest, rarest egg in the whole universe is right under your feet!"

"Egg white?" King Albu started to drool. "Goopo, taste it at once."

Goopo edged forwards, keeping his gun aimed at Teggs. He dipped a long finger in the goop, then sucked it clean.

At once, a dreamy smile spread over his face. "It – it's the best egg I've ever tasted!" he shrieked.

Goopo threw away his gun and dived into the sticky stream. It whooshed him right up to the top of the fountain. He balanced there, guzzling the liquid as if it was lemonade.

"Get out of that!" yelled King Albu. "It's mine!"

He jumped into the fountain, which
carried him high up into the air. He
and Goopo bobbed about on the thick
goo together, eating all they could.

"It's true!" shrieked the king. "It's the
eggiest egg-juice I ever tasted! Come
on, boys – tuck in!"

Prince Hibbit dived into the fountain
and the others followed him, crying for
joy. They were like mad birds flapping
about in a giant's birdbath.

All except
Prince Shelly. He
stood and stared
at his father and
brothers in horror.
"Stop it!" he
shouted. "You
heard Captain
Teggs – this whole
place is about to break
up! We must get out of here!"

But the oviraptors were far too busy
filling their faces to listen. They didn't
even notice when the fountain
suddenly got smaller . . .

"Albu! Goopo! Look out!" Teggs
yelled.

"Get out of there, you lot, quick!"
added Shelly.

But it was too late.

As quickly as it had come, the egg-
white fountain dried up to a dribble.
As the thick liquid fell away, for a

moment King Albu and his boys were left dangling in mid-air. Then, with a loud yell, they fell – right down into the deep hole.

"It must be miles down to the bottom!" said Arx.

They heard a quiet, distant splash. And then the scary wailing noise started up again. "Put me down!" they heard King Albu squawk in the distance. "I'll have you poached in butter for this!"

But then a terrible munching sound filled the air.

"The egg strikes back," said Teggs grimly.

"I tried to stop them," sighed Shelly.

"You did everything you could," Gipsy agreed.

"Come on," said Arx. "That thing is waking up, and it's hungry. We don't want to wind up as pudding!"

"You're right," said Teggs. "There's no time to lose."

"What about him?" Dippa scowled at Shelly. "If he comes with us he might eat our eggs!"

Shelly shook his head. "Believe me, I've lost my appetite!"

"Enough talk," yelled Teggs. "Back to the *Sauropod*! RUN!"

They ran for their lives.

The egg-planet rumbled and shook. Geysers of egg white spurted up all around them. The sky was darker than ever, and it was hard to see anything very clearly.

But somehow, they found their way back to the ship.

"Iggy!" yelled Teggs, panting for breath in the doorway. "Are you there?"

"Phew!" gasped Sog. "What's that terrible smell?"

"Must be Iggy and the boys," said Gipsy. "They've been working hard on our dung problem!"

Iggy appeared round the corner. He looked tired and red-faced, and his scaly hide was dripping with engine oil.

"We need to take off straight away," said Teggs. "Is that OK?"

Everyone stared at Iggy, hope burning in their eyes.

"Sorry, Captain," said Iggy, shaking his head. "We've got all the dung we need, but the engines are still stone-cold. And it'll take hours to burn enough dung for take-off!"

"But we don't *have* hours!" said Teggs.

Coo hung his head. The precious egg boxes fell to the floor. "Then . . . we can't escape!" he sighed. "It's all been for nothing!"

Chapter Ten

THE END OF THE EGG

"Wait a minute," said Dippa. "We can't take off, right?"

"Right," said Teggs.

She turned to Professor Sog. "And if we stay, we'll be flung off into space like you said, right?"

"It's true," he said sadly. "No one could survive such a thing."

"*We* certainly couldn't," Dippa agreed. "But maybe the *Sauropod* could – with us safely inside it!"

Arx hooted for joy. "She's right! There's still a chance! If this jumbo egg is going to hatch, we don't *need* to take off! The egg will launch us into space as it breaks up."

Teggs grinned at her. "Good thinking, Dippa." He turned to Iggy. "Do you think the *Sauropod* can stand it?"

Iggy shrugged. "She's a tough old ship . . . but I just don't know!"

"Well, I think we're about to find out," said Gipsy.

Just outside, a big split in the ground had opened up.

"Quick! Everyone to the flight deck!" yelled Teggs. "Find something to hold on to!"

Minutes later, the flight deck was filled to bursting with worried dinosaurs.

Iggy and his ankylosaurs had strapped themselves to the walls.

Gipsy, Teggs and Sog squashed up
together in the control pit. Arx sat at his
post, studying his instruments. Prince
Shelly sat nervously beside him. Dippa
and Coo huddled together, clinging to
their egg boxes. The alarm pterosaur
perched with the flight crew. She gave a
nervous squawk now and then.

Everyone had gathered together.
Perhaps for the last time.

Beneath the ship, the ground started to boil and buckle.

"Platus Two is cracking up," Arx reported.

"Hold tight, everybody," Teggs called. "And good luck."

They watched the egg-planet's last moments on the scanner screen.

The cracks in the ground grew wider and darker. They spat sticky goo high in the air. The *Sauropod* rattled and shook.

Then the distant horizon seemed to crack open. Something enormous burst out from beneath. It was groping around as if trying to grab the last stars in the sky.

"It's a claw!" cried Teggs. "A giant claw!"

More and more jagged cracks
appeared in the shaking shell.

"This is it!" cried Arx. "Here we go!"

And suddenly, there was a terrific
crack! as the egg-planet burst apart.

The scanner screen glowed white-hot.
The *Sauropod* was sent spinning. No
ship had ever stood up to such
incredible force.

"You can do it," Teggs whispered. "I know you can!"

And at last, after what seemed like hours and hours . . . the shaking and the spinning stopped.

For a long time no one moved. No one even dared to speak.

It was left to Teggs to break the silence. "We made it!" he shouted. "We actually made it!"

The flight deck rang with the sound of happy cheers and squawking.

Cautiously, Professor Sog wriggled out from Teggs's armpit. "Look!" he gasped. "On the screen!"

The blackness of space was littered with pieces of broken shell. They gleamed like bits of china in the starlight.

Then something incredible burst into view. It looked like an enormous winged serpent. Its gleaming, golden body stretched out through the stars like

a comet's tail. Slowly, it opened its jaws and breathed out a big ball of fire as bright as the sun.

"Wait a minute," said Arx. "That looks like . . ."

"It can't be!" gasped Sog.

"It is!" cried Teggs. "It's a star dragon, it must be! The Jurassic Explorers searched the galaxy, but never found one."

Arx beamed. "And now we've seen one with our own eyes!"

"In honour of my greatest heroes," said Teggs, "I name this star dragon Jurassic."

Jurassic the star dragon performed a slow somersault. Then she flapped away into the endless night on four massive, golden wings.

"I'm glad Jurassic hatched safely," said Gipsy softly. "I wonder where she'll go now?"

"To warm herself by a sun, perhaps," suggested Sog. "Or maybe to find her friends in a far-off galaxy. Who knows?"

Iggy smiled. "I'm sure there's a home big enough for her somewhere."

"Maybe we'll see her again some day," said Teggs happily. "And find out for sure."

They watched Jurassic slowly disappear, off on her long journey through the stars. Then Iggy disappeared too, to check on his precious engines.

"What about us? What about our home?" sighed Coo. "Where can we go with our eggs?"

Dippa smiled. "Cheer up, Coo. Like the star dragon – we'll find somewhere."

Prince Shelly hopped over. "I am so sorry for all the trouble my family caused you. Will you let me try to make it up to you?"

"Good for you, Shelly," said Teggs. "You're a very unusual oviraptor!"

"That's for sure," Shelly smiled. "To tell you the truth . . . eggs bring me

out in a rash!"

Arx chuckled. "Hey! You're now King Albu's only son. That makes *you* the king!"

"You're right!" Shelly said thoughtfully. "You know, my family owns a holiday moon near Pluto Springs. I went there once, as a hatchling – it's sunny and grassy and very quiet."

Dippa stared at him. "So?"

"So, I guess it's mine now." He smiled at her and Coo. "And I'd love to give it to you two! You can live there for as long as you like."

"Will we be safe from other oviraptors?" asked Coo.

"I promise," said Shelly. "King Albu's mad menus are a thing of the past. From now on, we'll leave you in peace!"

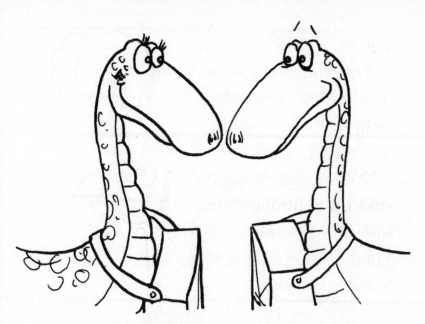

Dippa grinned at Coo. "Looks like we've got a new home out of this trip after all!"

Suddenly, the *Sauropod* lurched forwards. The sound of mighty engines firing filled the flight deck.

"Captain!" cried Iggy, jogging up to Teggs. "The heat of that explosion has warmed up the engines. We're ready to go back home!"

"First stop, Pluto Springs!" grinned Teggs.

"Oh, I do like a happy ending," cried Arx.

"Me too," said Gipsy, as she gave Prince Shelly a hug.

"And the really great thing about one mission ending is that a new mission is never far behind," said Teggs, beaming round at his fine crew. "Whatever it is — I hope it's just as *egg-citing* as this one!"

THE END

TALKING DINOSAUR

How to say the prehistoric
names in this book

STEGOSAURUS - STEG-oh-SORE-us

RAPTOR - RAP-tor

PTEROSAUR - teh-roh-SORE

DIMORPHODON - die_MORF-oh-don

TRICERATOPS - try-SERRA-tops

HADROSAUR - Had-roh-SORE

IGUANODON - ig-WHA-noh-don

ANKYLOSAUR - an-KILE-oh-SORE

Astrosaurs

THE MIND-SWAP
MENACE

by
Steve Cole

Illustrated by Woody Fox

RED FOX

To Alicia

Chapter One

SPACE WRECK

The spaceship was in a hurry. Shaped like an enormous metal egg, it shot past stars and planets at top speed.

Its name was the DSS *Sauropod*. It was the fastest ship in the Dinosaur Space Service.

It was on a vital mission.

And it was about to crash at ten million miles per hour into something that shouldn't be there at all . . .

"Red alert!" squawked the alarm pterosaur, the moment she noticed. Her screeching voice echoed throughout the *Sauropod*. "Unknown object ahead! We're going to crash! *Squaaaaawk!*"

"Hit the brakes!" yelled Captain Teggs Stegosaur from his control pit. "Fast!"

His flying reptile flight crew – fifty dynamic dimorphodon – flapped into action. Their claws closed on the brake levers. Their beaks bashed at the reverse rockets.

The *Sauropod* spun and skidded as it screeched to a halt. Teggs — an orange-brown stegosaurus — clamped his teeth round a huge clump of ferns and held on for dear life.

"Object straight ahead!" reported Gipsy, clinging to her chair. She was a stripy hadrosaur and was in charge of the ship's communications. "Can we steer around it?"

"Not while we're spinning like this," Teggs cried. "Arx, will we stop in time?"

"It's going to be close," Arx said. He was a wise and sturdy triceratops and Teggs's second-in-command. A dozen dimorphodon grabbed hold of his horns to stop him sliding away from his controls. "Oh, no!

The brakes are burning out!"

"Don't worry, they won't let us down," cried Iggy, hanging onto a safety rail. This tough iguanodon was the *Sauropod*'s chief engineer. He knew the ship like the back of his claw. "I built those brakes myself! They can handle worse than this."

"You mean it can *get* worse than this?" cried Gipsy. Her head-crest flushed bright blue with alarm.

At last, with a final flip, the *Sauropod* came to a stop.

"I told you we'd make it," grinned Iggy.

"It was close, though," said Arx, as a dimorphodon wiped sweat from his frilly forehead.

"Switch on the scanner!" cried Teggs. "Let's see what's out there!"

More dimorphodon flocked to obey. On the screen, Teggs and his crew could see something that looked like a big, silver wheel, slowly spinning.

"Looks like a space station of some kind," said Arx.

"It's not on any of the space maps," said Gipsy. "I've sent a greetings message but there's no reply."

Teggs pointed at the screen with his spiky tail. "Maybe *that* would explain why!"

A huge, black, jagged hole had been torn in the outside of the space station.

"This is a wheel with a puncture," said Iggy. "Must be a space wreck!"

"It doesn't look very old," said Gipsy. "I wonder where it came from?"

"I don't recognize the design," said Arx. But as the wheel kept turning, he suddenly saw a blood-red sign on the silver surface. It was a dinosaur skull with rows of jagged teeth.

A shiver crept up the long, bony spines of the astrosaurs. They all knew that this design was the mark of meat-eaters.

"It's a carnivore space station!" cried Iggy. "What's it doing here in the Vegetarian Sector?"

"It could be a trick," Gipsy suggested. "Maybe some meat-eaters are sneakily trying to invade us."

"There are no other ships nearby," said Arx. "It's more likely that this wreck has just drifted across from their side of space into ours."

"Well, we can't just leave it here," said Teggs. "It's a danger to passing ships. Let's zip across and set up a beacon there, like a lighthouse in space, warning other travellers away."

Arx cleared his scaly throat. "Excuse me, sir, but can we spare the time? We *are* in the middle of a mercy mission."

Teggs had not forgotten. On the planet Diplos, whole herds of starving diplodocus needed help fast. A freak hailstorm had wiped out their harvest.

The *Sauropod* had been loaded up with plants and seeds so the dinosaurs could feed again.

"I think this is important, Arx," said Teggs. "What if *another* ship on *another* important mission crashes into this thing? That could lead to total disaster!"

Arx bowed his head. "You're quite right, Captain," he said. "I'm sorry."

"Nothing to be sorry about," smiled Teggs. "Now, I'd better go and get the beacon."

"I'll get the shuttle ready!" said Iggy, bounding off to the lift.

Teggs reared up out of the control pit. "We won't be long. Warm up the engines and be ready to zoom off to Diplos the moment we're back on board."

"We'll be ready, sir," Gipsy promised.

Arx said nothing, his eyes glued to the scanner screen. He wished Teggs and Iggy didn't have to go. He had a niggling feeling in his bones that this sinister space wreck spelled danger.

It took less than a minute for the shuttle to reach the space station. Teggs and Iggy climbed in through the air lock. They found themselves in a gloomy corridor.

"Let's have a quick look around," said Teggs. "Just in case anyone has been hurt."

"If there are any meat-eaters still on this station, *we* could get hurt!" said Iggy. Even so, he followed his captain

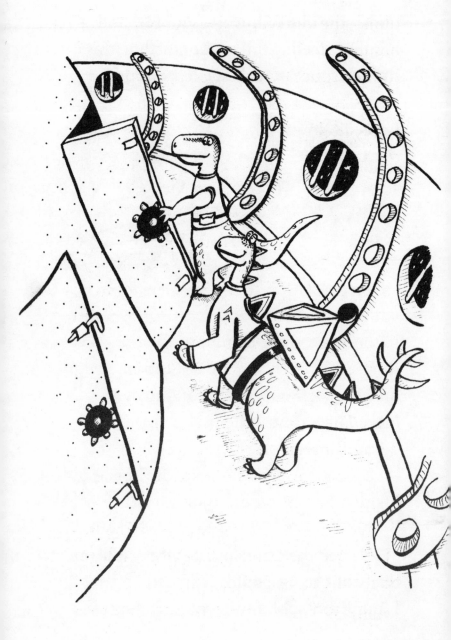

along the dark passage without hesitation.

The station was a grim, forbidding place. It was made of metal and thick with shadows. To their right, stars shone a ghostly light through small, barred windows in the outer wall. To their left was a line of heavy doors, covered in bolts and locks.

Teggs tried one of them. The door creaked open onto a cramped room with just a bed and a bucket inside. It looked like some kind of jail cell.

"Iggy? I think this place was a prison," said Teggs. "A lockup for carnivore criminals!"

Iggy agreed. "Pretty *dangerous* criminals, too, from the size of those locks!"

"We won't hang about," said Teggs. "Let's get the beacon working and go back to the *Sauropod*."

Iggy took the bulky beacon from his

captain's back and set it up in the cell. It looked like a large red triangle with a transmitter on the top.

"There," said Iggy. "That will send out a recorded message telling any passing ships to keep out of the way."

Teggs grinned at him. "Next stop, Diplos! Come on."

But the cell door wouldn't open.

"Funny," said Teggs. "Must be stuck."

"But we left it open so we could move about!" Iggy remembered. "There's hardly room in

here to swing a compsognathus!"

Teggs nodded grimly. "So either it swung shut behind us and jammed – or someone has locked us in!"

A nasty snigger came from the other side of the door. Then a white, wispy gas started pumping through the keyhole.

"Hold your breath, Iggy!" Teggs gasped. "We've walked into a trap!"

Chapter Two

THE MIND-SWAPPER

"It's too late, Captain," choked Iggy, clutching at his throat as the gas engulfed him. "I'm getting dizzy . . ." He fell face-first onto the ground, his short, stiff tail pointing up in the air.

Teggs bashed his body against the

door with all his strength. But it was no good. The door was too strong, and the gas was making him weak.

As he slipped to the floor beside Iggy, he rolled over and squashed the beacon flat.

Gipsy had been listening to the beacon's signal. "The warning's coming out loud and clear," she told Arx, happily.

But then the signal stopped dead.

"What happened?" asked Arx.

"I don't know," said Gipsy. "Maybe the beacon is faulty." She tried to get Teggs on the communicator. "Captain Teggs, this is Gipsy. Is everything OK?"

There was no reply.

"Come on, Gipsy," said Arx. "Let's get over there. I've got a bad feeling about that place."

Gipsy told the dimorphodon to look after the control room until they returned, then followed Arx over to the lift. "You think Teggs and Iggy could be in trouble, don't you?"

"I only hope I'm wrong," sighed Arx.

But Gipsy knew that Arx was rarely wrong about anything.

Slowly, Teggs woke up. He ached from the tip of his tail to the bottom of his beak. His head felt like it was full of extra-smelly dung, and his mouth was as dry as a desert.

He opened his eyes to find himself lying on his side in a large, well-lit room. A big TV buzzed in the corner, its screen full of static. How did he get there?

Suddenly he remembered the gas, and the evil snigger from behind the cell door.

"Iggy!" he cried. "Iggy, are you all right?"

"I think so," gasped Iggy weakly from somewhere behind him. "But I can't move!"

Teggs tried to kick his legs. "I can't move either. I've been tied up!"

"You have indeed, you pair of plant-eating potatoes," said a sinister voice nearby. "My home-made sleep

gas made it easy-peasy. You are now in my power! Aren't they, Ardul?"

"Yes, sir, Mr Boss." This second voice sounded altogether more stupid. "They is in your clutches, and that is the truth."

"What do you want with us?" Teggs demanded, struggling to free his legs. "Who are you? Where are we?"

There was a quiet thud and a scampering sound. Suddenly, a mean little dinosaur with goblin eyes and rows of sharp teeth was standing over Teggs's head. "Good afternoon," he hissed. "You are in the prison officers' lounge."

"Are you prison officers, then?" Teggs asked.

"We used to be *prisoners* – but soon we shall be free dinosaurs again!" The mean little meat-eater chuckled and his thick friend quickly joined in. "My name is Dasta — Crool Dasta, the sneakiest coelophysis ever!"

"Crool Dasta?!" gasped Teggs.

Dasta flashed an evil smile. "You've heard of me, then?"

"No," Teggs admitted. "I just can't believe you've got such a stupid name."

"I happen to be an evil inventor and a criminal genius," said Dasta snootily.

"You can't be *that* clever," said Teggs. "Otherwise you wouldn't have been caught! Or did your stupid sidekick mess things up for you?"

At that, Ardul came running up to him. Ardul was another coelophysis — shorter, fatter and twice as ugly as his boss.

"Don't speak to us that way," said Ardul. "You is dating on thin ice."

"You mean *skating* on thin ice, Ardul," sighed Dasta.

"Where's everyone else?" Iggy asked.

"This prison was almost destroyed when a meteor crashed into it," hissed Dasta. "Everyone else got away. The prison officers thought that Ardul and I were killed in the explosion – but we were only hiding!"

"Neat trick," said Teggs. "How long have you been hanging out on this space wreck?"

"Three months," the carnivore confessed. "But I knew that one day we would drift into the path of another ship – and we would be free once more! Free to collect our secret treasure from the Geldos Cluster and live like kings!"

"Free?" Teggs scoffed. "Come off it.

142

You may have caught us, but you're still stuck here."

"I don't think so," sniggered Dasta. "Your crew will be getting worried. They will come to get you. But what they'll get is *us*, Ardul and me – and they won't even know it!"

Teggs felt worried all of a sudden. "What are you talking about?"

"Take a look at your ugly friend and find out," Dasta snorted.

Teggs rolled over backwards to see. "Iggy!" he cried. "You're wearing some weird contraption on your head!"

"So are *you*, Captain," said Iggy nervously.

Dasta gave a gurgling laugh. Then he placed a similar helmet on his own head. Ardul did the same.

"The helmets are connected to my latest brilliant invention," Dasta explained, pointing to a menacing machine full of buttons and coloured lights. "It's a mind-swapper! It will put my brain in your body, Captain Teggs, and Ardul's brain into Iggy's!"

Teggs gulped. "What happens to *our* brains?"

"They is gonna be sucked into *our* 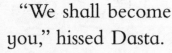 bodies," said Ardul, with a cruel grin.

"We shall become you," hissed Dasta.

"And you shall become us! Your foolish friends will take us back to your ship – and we'll take over!"

"No!" cried Teggs.

"Yes," laughed Dasta. "Ardul, start the machine!"

The mind-swapper began to throb and hiss and steam. Blue electric light crackled all around it. Then it made a nasty sucking noise, like a slug trying to swallow a boiled sweet.

Teggs cried out. His brain felt on fire.
Dasta laughed and clapped as the
machine sucked harder and harder . . .

Chapter Three

STRANDED IN SPACE

With a loud POP! it was all over.

Teggs found he could move.
Confused, he got to his feet. But he
was no longer a massive, powerful,
seven-ton stegosaur. Now he was a
zippy, nippy little monster, as light as a
feather. His mind had been plopped
into Dasta's body!

And Dasta, meanwhile had taken Teggs's form. "My invention works perfectly!" he cried. "Everyone will think I'm Captain Teggs of the DSS!"

"Iggy?" the real Teggs asked. His voice came out as a nasty little hiss. "Iggy, tell me you're still you!"

But his old friend only sniggered. "I is not Iggy!" he said. "I is Ardul!"

"His mind's taken over my body, Captain," said the real Iggy. "While

I'm stuck as the ugliest coelophysis in the galaxy! What are we going to do?"

"We have to reverse the mind-swap!" cried Teggs. "They're still tied up, they can't stop us!"

"Only *I* can swap our minds back again," jeered Dasta. "You'll never work out how it's done!"

Teggs stared at the controls and tried to think. But being in someone else's body was very distracting. He clicked his long, pointed claws together. He ran his tongue over his sharp teeth – and nearly sliced it off. There was a horrible taste in his mouth – raw meat! He was almost sick at the thought of it.

Suddenly the door burst open, and Gipsy and Arx rushed in.

"Arx! Gipsy!" cried the real Teggs in delight. "You're here!"

Gipsy frowned. "Who in space are *you?*"

"You wicked little meat-eaters," snarled Arx. "How dare you tie up our friends!"

"*We're* your friends!" wailed the real Iggy, jumping up and down in his bogus body. "Not them!"

But Arx and Gipsy ignored him.
Straight away, they started
untying the *fake* Teggs
and Iggy!

"Please,
listen!" the real
Teggs begged
them in his new,
hissy voice. "We
may look like mean
carnivores, but I'm
really your
captain – and he
is the real Iggy! Our
minds have been put in the wrong
bodies, that's all!"

"Ridiculous!" cried Dasta. "What a
silly story."

And Arx believed him, of course,
because he looked and sounded just
like Teggs.

"Now come on, Arx, get your beak

moving on those ropes. Ahhh!" Dasta winked at the real Teggs. "Free at last!"

"That is better!" cried Ardul, as Gipsy untied his ropes and he got to his feet. "*Much* better!"

"You're making a big mistake!" cried the real Teggs. "Arx, *please*—"

But before he could say anything else, Dasta lashed out with his long stegosaur tail – and sent him flying into the real Iggy. Both the little dinosaurs ended up in a dazed heap in the corner.

Dasta chuckled. He liked this new body — it was full of power!

"Was that necessary, Captain?" Arx frowned.

"Don't feel sorry for him," said the fake Teggs. "That's Crool Dasta — the cleverest crook in the cosmos. I expect you've heard of me. Er . . . him. Haven't you?"

"No," said Arx.

Dasta sighed. "Well, anyway, he and his friend have been stuck on this space wreck for months, and it must have turned their brains funny. All this talk of swapping minds and bodies . . . Ha!"

"What does this gadget do?" asked Gipsy, pointing to the mind-swapper.

"It's a terrible torture device," Dasta lied. "First, they gassed us. Then they tied us up. If you hadn't saved us, I don't know *what* would have happened." He reared up, eager to be off. "Now come on, we must be going!"

Arx frowned. "Don't you want to set up another beacon here?"

"No time!" he cried. "We're in a rush!"

"Very well," said Arx. "I suppose we'd better take these crooks with us. We can drop them off at DSS Headquarters on our way back from Diplos."

"This pair aren't going anywhere," said Dasta. "Deal with them, er . . . Iggy?"

The fake Iggy marched over to the
little dinosaurs and grabbed them by
their tails. Then he shoved them both
down the rubbish chute! A moment
later, the mind-swap machine was
stuffed down after them.

"Iggy, what are you doing!" cried
Gipsy. "Whatever they've done, we
can't just leave those dinosaurs here!"

"Of course we can," said Dasta.

"Now, lead the way back to our ship.
And that's an order!"

Arx nodded slowly. "Yes, Captain."

As Arx and Gipsy led the way, Dasta
turned to Ardul. "I think I'm going to
enjoy being a spaceship captain," he
hissed. "From now on, my mind is

staying in *this* body."

"I is gonna enjoy being an iggu-nana, too," said Ardul. "But I is not liking the thought of eating plants."

Dasta sniggered. "When these fools have taken us to the Geldos Cluster, they'll be of no more use to us." He licked his new, stegosaurus lips. "And then we'll eat the lot of them!"

Sprawled on a big heap of rubbish, the real Teggs opened his eyes. All around was dark and slimy and stank of rotten meat.

"Iggy?" he hissed. "Are you there?"

There was a clattering from the pile beside him. "Just about," Iggy groaned.

"I've never been hit by my own tail before," said Teggs, ruefully. "That body of mine packs quite a punch, doesn't it!"

"What are we going to do, Captain?" Iggy whispered.

Teggs reached out a claw and patted him on the shoulder. "Don't worry," he said. "We'll find a way out of this."

But then, a deep rumbling sounded from the darkness. The rotten rubbish they were sitting on started to tremble and shake.

Teggs stared around blindly. "What's that?"

"I'd know that noise anywhere," said Iggy. "It's engines. The *Sauropod* shuttle's engines!"

"Then . . ." Teggs swallowed, "then they're leaving us behind!"

"We'll never see our friends again," said Iggy, sadly. "And we'll *never* get our bodies back!"

Chapter Four

NO ESCAPE

Dasta enjoyed the walk from the
Sauropod's shuttle bay to the flight deck.
Everyone he passed thought he was
really Teggs, and they all smiled and
saluted. Clearly, Teggs was a popular
captain.

"He won't be for much longer,"
chuckled Dasta.

Gipsy and Arx led him on to the flight deck. Ardul was right behind him. Unfortunately, he was finding it harder than Dasta to get used to his new body. He kept walking into doors and walls.

"Iggy, mind out!" said Gipsy. "You'll bring the whole place crashing down."

"I is just, um, a bit dizzy after breathing in the grass," said Ardul.

"*Gas*, you idiot!" cried Dasta. "They didn't leave us on a lawn, did they?"

"If you're not feeling well, Iggy, maybe you should lie down in your room," Arx suggested.

"Sounds good," said Ardul. "Where *is* my room?"

Gipsy frowned. "I'll get one of the dimorphodon to take you there. Try to get some sleep!"

She whistled to a dimorphodon and it flapped off into the lift. Ardul followed, drooling.

"Don't eat it, you idiot," whispered Dasta. "Or they'll know for sure you aren't the real Iggy!"

"It is a juicy looking flapper," sighed Ardul, as the lift doors closed behind him. "But I will try."

"Ready to go, Captain," said Arx. "Full speed ahead to Diplos?"

"Diplos? Get real!" Dasta snorted. He stumbled into Teggs's control pit and tried to look natural. "Steer this ship to the Geldos Cluster."

"Geldos?" Arx blinked. "But that's in meat-eater space!"

"So?"

"So, we're plant-eaters!" Gipsy protested. "We can't just enter the Carnivore Sector without permission! They might think we are invading!"

"Well, we'll worry about that when the time comes," said Dasta. "Head for the Geldos Cluster – now!"

"Why?" asked Arx. "What's so important? What about all those poor dinosaurs  starving on Diplos?"

Dasta peered at him from the pit. "Who is your captain, Arx?" he said quietly.

Arx stiffened. "*You* are, sir."

"Then do as I say, you tiresome triceratops!" he bellowed. "Now!"

Gipsy felt her legs wobble as Arx changed the *Sauropod*'s course through space. She had never, ever heard Teggs shout at his first officer before. What was the matter with him? Could the gas have affected him more than they'd thought?

Teggs was acting like a totally different dinosaur . . .

★

Back on the prison, the real Teggs and Iggy were trying to find their way out of the slippery, slimy rubbish heap, carefully carrying the mind-swapper. They moved slowly at first, not used to their new, unfamiliar bodies. But soon they were climbing nimbly through the rubbish pile towards a faint, ghostly light.

"Where's it coming from?" asked Iggy.

"It's coming from the end of this chute," Teggs reported. He patted a filthy metal pipe. "If we can climb up this thing, we'll reach that light."

"What does it matter?" sighed Iggy. "We're trapped here for ever, inside these silly little bodies – while Dasta and Ardul lead the *Sauropod* off to find their secret treasure!"

"We'll get our bodies back," said Teggs. "After all, we've still got the mind-swapper. There's still hope!"

After a lot of scrabbling about, they found themselves at the top of the rubbish chute. A glass lid blocked their way out but

 Teggs found he was able to use his claws to prise it open.

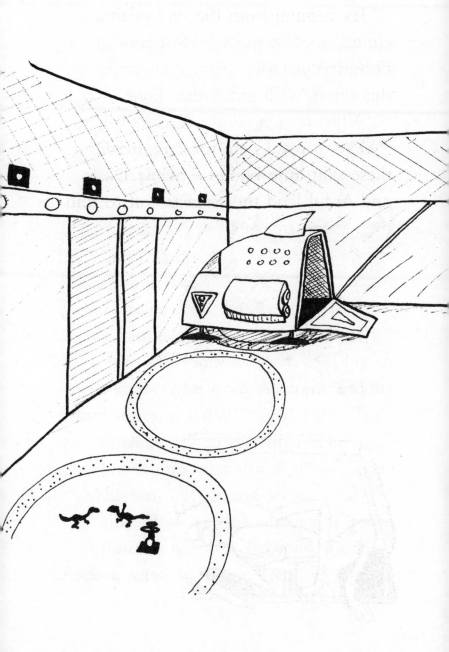

Iggy crawled out after him, carrying the mind-swap machine. "Where are we now?" he asked.

Teggs looked around. They were in a large, echoing chamber, which was dimly lit by a single light bulb. It was empty except for one thing – a spaceship.

"This must be the prison's docking bay!" cried Teggs. "When everyone else evacuated, I guess that ship wasn't needed – so it was left behind!"

"Maybe it doesn't work," said Iggy, trying not to get too excited.

"You'll soon get it going again," Teggs told him. "You're brilliant with engines!"

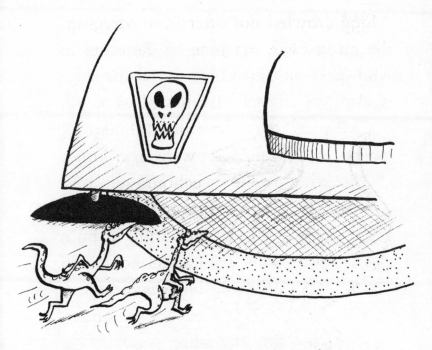

The two of them ran across the deserted shuttle bay to inspect the ship.

"It looks all right," said Iggy. "Tip-top, in fact. Which strikes me as strange."

"Why?" asked Teggs.

"Well, Dasta's clever with machines too," he said. "So why didn't he just get on this ship with Ardul and take off for the Geldos Cluster months ago?"

"Maybe he didn't know it was here," Teggs argued, climbing up the steps to the spaceship. He threw open the door.

And an ear-splitting alarm went off.

"Maybe!" gasped Iggy. "Or maybe he knew *that* would happen!"

"So what!" said Teggs. "It's only an alarm. There's no one left to hear it!"

But Teggs was wrong.

A hidden door in the wall slid open. And something truly terrifying came out.

Clanking and steaming, a line of massive mechanical T. rexes trooped into the docking bay. Each one was the size of a *Sauropod* shuttle. Their red laser eyes swept all about the room.

"Now we know why Dasta and Ardul didn't take this ship," gasped Iggy. "The prison officers must use these things as guards!"

"Just as scary as real T. rexes," Teggs agreed. "But much easier to train, and

less likely to eat the crooks they're
guarding!"

"*Prisoners escaping*," said the robot T.
rex leader in a jerky voice. "*Prisoners
identified as Dasta and Ardul.*"

"We're not!" shouted Teggs. "We're
peaceful astrosaurs! We're just trapped
in their rotten bodies!"

But the computerized carnivores weren't listening. They started clanking towards the shuttle. "*Escaping prisoners must be destroyed!*" they roared. "*Kill them! Kill them both!*"

Teggs and Iggy stared helplessly as the T. rex robots closed in.

Chapter Five

THE ENEMY WITHIN

"Look out!" yelled Teggs, as the nearest robot T. rex fired laser beams from its glowing eyes. He grabbed Iggy by the arm and dragged him out of the way. The blast struck the side of the ship, which went up in smoke.

"Thanks, Teggs!" said Iggy. "That was close!"

"We've got one tiny chance," Teggs said. "Our new bodies are smaller and faster than our normal ones. That'll make us harder to hit."

Another blast of ruby light burned into the ground beside them. Teggs and

Iggy ran for their lives, zigzagging across the floor. But more and more laser beams came zapping from the

metal creatures' eyes.

"We can't dodge them for ever!" gasped Iggy.

Teggs nodded, and felt the searing heat of a death ray sizzle past his head. "Change of plan. Follow me!"

To Iggy's amazement, Teggs sprinted *towards* the nearest killer robot! He ducked in and out of the monster's massive metal feet. Terrified, Iggy ran after him and joined in the dangerous dance.

"It can't shoot us when we're almost underneath it," Teggs explained.

"But its friends can!" cried Iggy. Even now, more robots were closing in.

"Get ready to dodge when I do,"
Teggs told him. "NOW!"

He and Iggy ducked away from the
robot's legs just as four of the T. rexes
opened fire. The blast blew up the
creature's ankles. With a great robotic
roar, it crashed to the ground.

"One down, seven to go!" gasped
Teggs. "We have to stay ahead of
them!"

Suddenly, Iggy had an idea. "Or just
stay on their heads!" he shouted. "What
do you think? These little bodies of
ours should be good for climbing."

"I'm game if you are," said Teggs.

Together, they darted over to the
nearest robot. It tried to stamp on
them, but they were too fast and
jumped on its tail. It tried to shake
them off, but they were already
climbing up its mechanical backbone.

"Why are we heading for the head?"
asked Teggs.

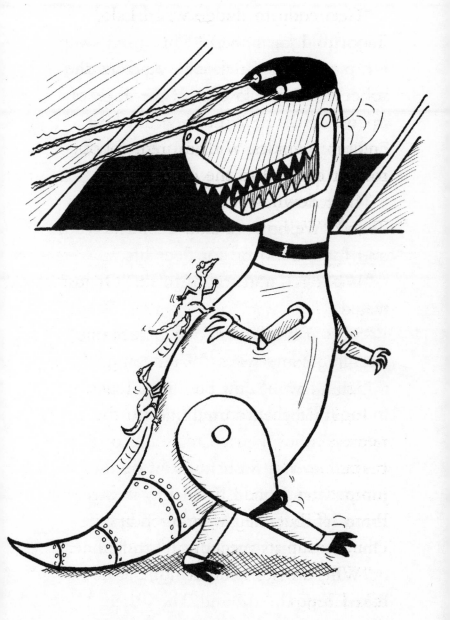

"I want to do some robot brain surgery!" Iggy smiled. "This mind swap has put me in the mood!" And he dug his coelophysis claws into the back of the robot's head. A moment later he had ripped away a metal panel and pulled out the wires within.

The robot bucked like a deranged donkey, trying to shake them off. Teggs and Iggy clung on for dear life.

"What are you trying to do?" Teggs yelled.

"Start a brainstorm," Iggy explained, wiggling some wires. "With any luck, this thing won't just be after us any more. It'll be after anything that moves!"

There was a flash from inside the robot's metal head. Suddenly, it was firing its lasers at the other T. rexes! One burst into flames and crashed against its neighbour, bringing it burning to the ground. The other

T. rexes fired back wildly, hitting each other as well as the rebel robot. Their metal bodies were soon scorched and smoking. One by one they exploded in a blaze of sparks and went crashing to the ground.

When the chaos was over, Teggs and Iggy were still clinging to their rebel-robot's scrambled circuits. It looked around for anything else to

fight – but found nothing. Slowly, the
lights in its eyes flickered out. Then, it
began to sway from side to side.

"Get ready to jump!" cried Teggs, as
the robot finally toppled over.

At the last possible moment, he and
Iggy jumped clear. The robot smashed
into the ground – and they skidded

safely on their bottoms to the far side of the smoky shuttle bay.

"We made it!" whooped Iggy. "We actually made it!"

"We did," Teggs agreed. "But I'm not sure the ship was so lucky!"

Iggy's smile soon vanished as the smoke started to clear. Now he could see that the shuttle had been well and truly zapped. It had more holes in it than a Swiss cheese.

"I hope you can fix that ship, Iggy," said Teggs. "Because if you can't, we'll be stuck here for good!"

Gipsy was worried. Her captain was acting very strangely. First, he ordered them to fly into the Carnivore Sector. Then he said he was going off to take a nap. Teggs *never* napped on duty.

While Arx sat at his controls in a sulk, Gipsy decided to visit Iggy. She would ask him *exactly* what happened

on board the space wreck. Perhaps he would remember something that might explain Teggs's odd behaviour.

But as she neared Iggy's room, she stopped. She could hear voices. Teggs was in there, talking to Iggy. He wasn't having a nap at all!

Gipsy pressed her ear up against the door.

"We'll be coming up to the Carnivore Sector any time now," Teggs was saying. "From there, it should only take a few hours to reach Geldos."

"I isn't thinking I can last that long!"
Iggy roared.

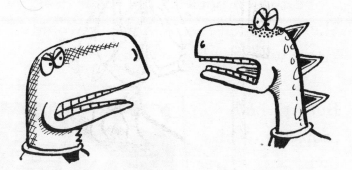

Why was he talking so strangely?
Gipsy wondered.

"I is needing fresh meat! Let me eat
just one of them flappers."

"No!" said Teggs.

"There is lots of them about! No one
will miss just one!"

"I said no! You're supposed to be an
iguanodon. Eat some more ferns."

"Ferns taste of poo," Iggy grumbled.
"Can't we just get *one* flapper? I will
only nibble its beak, promise!"

Gipsy gasped and jumped away from

the door. Something was *very* wrong. Just what had happened to Teggs and Iggy on that space wreck?

She rushed back to the flight deck. She would tell Arx. Maybe *he* would know what to do.

But Arx had problems of his own.

The *Sauropod* had been in the Carnivore Sector less than two minutes when a scary ship came whizzing into view. It was blood-red and shaped like a huge, jagged tooth, gleaming in the starlight.

"A raptor death ship," breathed Arx. It was the biggest he'd ever seen. He jabbed the red alert button with his nose horn and the alarm pterosaur started squawking wildly.

"Captain Teggs, Gipsy, this is Arx. Please report to the flight deck! Iggy, get to the engine room, quick!"

Gipsy arrived seconds later. "I was just on my way to see you," she said. "What's up?" Then she saw the death ship on the scanner and her head-crest flushed bright blue. "Arx, they're sending us a message!"

"I suppose we'd better hear it then," said Arx gravely.

Gipsy flicked a switch. A sinister hissing voice sounded from the  speakers. "Thisss is the Raptor Border Patrol," it said. "You have entered the Carnivore Sssector without permission. Prepare to be destroyed!"

Chapter Six

CHASE THROUGH SPACE

The dimorphodon flapped about in alarm. Arx swallowed hard. "This is the DSS *Sauropod*," he said. "Please do not open fire. We are here on an urgent mission! At least, I *think* it's urgent."

"What isss thisss mission?" demanded the raptors.

Arx turned to Gipsy helplessly. "What do I tell them? I don't know *what* we're doing here!"

Suddenly the lift doors opened and Teggs appeared — or rather, Dasta appeared in Teggs's body. "Why the red alert?" he asked.

"We're about to be blown up by a raptor death ship, Captain," said Arx. "They want to know what we're doing here."

"Stupid raptors, sticking their snouts in," said Dasta. "It's none of their business!"

"*We* would like to know too," Gipsy said firmly.

"How dare you question your own captain?" Dasta roared. "Now let's just blast these raptors and get on with it!"

Arx stared at him in horror. "We can't just open fire on a raptor border patrol! That is an act of war!"

"And disobeying me is *mutiny*, Arx!" said Dasta. "Fire cannons, torpedoes, everything. All at once!"

Arx rushed over to the fake Teggs, still unaware that an evil carnivore had borrowed his captain's body. "Please, Captain," he said. "It's not called a death ship for nothing! They could destroy us!"

"Thisss isss your last chance," hissed the raptors through the *Sauropod*'s speakers. "Explain yourselves or die!"

"We have to fire first," said Dasta. He gave Arx a crafty smile. "Trust me, Arx. Have I ever let you down before?"

"No," Arx admitted. "Never."

He wanted to believe in his captain, more than anything.

Gipsy waited nervously. Would Arx do what he was told?

At last, he told the dimorphodon: "Very well. Fire everything as the captain says."

The flying reptiles flapped off to obey. They fired lasers, cannons and dung torpedoes. The death ship shook and lurched to one side as the weapons found their mark.

But then it straightened up, and started speeding towards them.

"Was that the best we could do?" complained Dasta. "Rubbish!"

"Plant-eating ssscum!" the raptors hissed. "Prepare to die!"

"Well, if we can't shoot them down, we'd better run!" said Dasta grumpily. "But stay on course for Geldos!"

"Full speed ahead!" shouted Arx.

The *Sauropod* sped away. But the death ship was right behind them. It opened fire, and the *Sauropod* rocked with the blast.

"They've blown off our lasers!" said Arx.

"They're gaining on us!" cried Gipsy.

"Go faster!" snapped Dasta.

"We can't!" Arx said. "Not unless Iggy boosts the engines!"

"I'll call him," said Gipsy. She flicked a switch. "Iggy? Iggy, we need you to boost the engines!"

"Hang on, stripy girl." It sounded like Iggy, but of course it was really Ardul. "I is just trying to find the engine room."

"Iggy, what's wrong with you?" she wailed.

"I is fine," he said. "But what does an engine look like again?"

Arx frowned. "He's gone crazy!"

"Just a touch of brain flu," said Dasta. "He's been looking a bit peaky lately, don't you think?"

"Well, Captain," said Gipsy coldly. "I certainly noticed he wasn't himself."

The *Sauropod* shook as another blast hit home.

"Our cannons have been hit!" cried Gipsy.

"There's just one chance!" Arx shouted. "Perhaps if we dump all our dung torpedoes . . ."

"*Dump* them?" Dasta roared. "That will leave us at their mercy!"

"Not if we dump them right in their path!" grinned Gipsy.

"Exactly," said Arx. "Let's do it."

Gipsy whistled at the dimorphodon. They flapped off eagerly and set to work.

"Ready for dumping . . . now!" cried Gipsy.

Arx hit a button, and fifty dung torpedoes dropped out of the *Sauropod*'s bottom.

The raptor death ship was going too

fast to stop. It flew right into the astrosaurs' trap! The torpedoes all went off together in one big bang . . .

And when it was over, the death ship had become
a *dung*
ship! It no
longer
looked
like a big,
scary
tooth –
just a
massive,
smelly dung
ball!

The
dimorphodon
clapped and
cheered, and Gipsy slapped Arx on the back proudly.

"That should slow the raptors down," she said. "Good thinking, Arx."

"Yes, well," said Dasta sniffily. "A very clever plan, I'm sure."

"You should know, Captain," said Arx. "You *invented* that plan."

Dasta gulped. "I did?"

"Yes, in your final space exam," said Arx, advancing slowly. "Admiral Rosso was so impressed by your quick thinking, he made you the captain of the *Sauropod* straight away."

"Or rather, he made *Teggs* the captain of the *Sauropod*," said Gipsy. "But you're *not* Teggs, are you? Just like Iggy isn't Iggy. You're both imposters!"

"Nonsense, girl!" snarled Dasta. "Of course I'm Teggs! You must be spacesick!"

"The real Teggs would never have risked our lives like that," Gipsy argued. "And the real Iggy knows what an engine looks like!"

"You've been acting funny ever since we rescued you," said Arx. "At first I thought that the gas on the space prison had made you ill. But now I think you must actually be Crool Dasta and his sidekick. You have put your minds in the bodies of our friends!"

"You're crazy!" cried Dasta.

"It explains a lot," said Gipsy. "I heard them talking in Iggy's room, Arx. They were talking about eating the dimorphodon!"

At this, the dimorphodon shrieked and cheeped and fluttered.

"Why would we want to eat them?" Dasta protested. "There's not enough meat on them!"

Arx and Gipsy gasped in horror.
Dasta realized he had said too much.

"So, *that's* why Iggy stuck those two
coelophysis down the rubbish chute,"
said Gipsy. "To stop them convincing us
of who you really were! Those nasty
little dinosaurs used to be *you*, before
you swapped minds. Now they're Teggs
and Iggy!"

"Well done, you sap-swallowing
fools!" The fake Teggs jumped out of the

control pit. "You worked it out at last. I *am* the one and only Crool Dasta!"

"Then I'm turning round, right now," said Arx.

"No!" Dasta cried.

"Yes," Arx insisted. "The starving dinosaurs of Diplos *need* the food we're carrying. We'll rescue the real Teggs and Iggy on the way."

"And then you are going to put their minds back in their own bodies," Gipsy warned Dasta. "Or else!"

Just then, the lift doors opened and Ardul came out. "Is this the engine room?" he asked.

"Never mind that, Ardul!" snapped Dasta. "Grab the girl!"

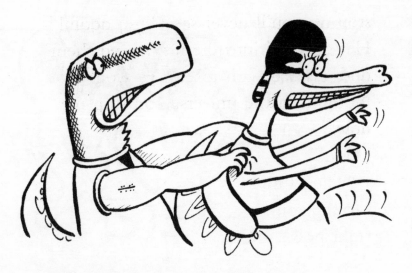

Gipsy gasped as the fake Iggy
yanked her arm.

"Let her go!" said Arx. He lowered
his head, ready to charge.

"Stay back," hissed Dasta. "Or we'll
do something *very* nasty to your
friend. Come on, Ardul, let's get out of
here."

"Yes, sir, Mr Boss-Captain," said
Ardul. He bundled Gipsy into the lift.

"Go ahead and turn this ship round,
Arx," Dasta cried. "We'll take a shuttle
to Geldos from here. And if you try to

stop us, you'll never see Gipsy again!"
He squeezed into the lift behind them
and cackled with glee. "I've won!
Nothing in the universe can stop me
now!"

Chapter Seven

THE TREASURE OF GELDOS

Gipsy tried to escape, but Ardul's grip was too strong. Dasta led them to the nearest shuttle and she was thrown inside.

"Why are you doing all this?" she demanded, rubbing her bruised arm.

"What is so important about the Geldos Cluster?"

"A great treasure is hidden there," said Dasta. He started the shuttle's engines. "The most valuable invention in the world!"

"Invented by you?"

"Of course!" he snapped. "Before Ardul and I were arrested, I managed to hide it on a tiny planet in the middle of the Cluster."

"What were you arrested for, anyway?" asked Gipsy.

"My invention was very expensive to build," said Dasta. "I had to rob the Universal Raptor Bank to pay for the parts. That's why I teamed up with Ardul."

Ardul nodded proudly. "I is the best rank slobber in space."

"The best *bank robber*, you dino-nut. And I only wish you were!" The shuttle took off in a cloud of stinky smoke. "Ardul here forgot to wear his robber's mask," Dasta explained. "He was recognized. The raptor police tracked him down – and me with him!"

"Good," said Gipsy. But she had to admit she was curious. "What *is* this incredible invention, anyway?"

"The replicator," said Dasta proudly. "It makes a perfect copy of anything you put inside it. Gold . . . jewels . . . anything at all!"

Gipsy gasped. "That *is* amazing!"

Dasta pulled a gold piece from his belt. "All I need is a single coin, and I can make a million more . . ."

"That is what you is promising to pay me for slobbing that rank," grumbled Ardul. "One million gold pieces."

"And that's what you shall get, my friend," said Dasta. "When the replicator is mine once again!"

"So where exactly did you hide it?" Gipsy asked.

"On Geldos Beta," said Dasta. He

peered at the shuttle's controls. "In this little tub, we should reach there in just over two hours!"

Gipsy glanced down at her communicator. What Dasta didn't know was that she had secretly switched it on. Every word of their conversation had been transmitted to Arx back on the *Sauropod*.

But was there anything Arx could do?

★

On the flight deck, Arx listened gravely to Dasta's boasting. The dimorphodon were perched all over him, twittering and flapping in dismay. Arx was glad of their company. With Teggs, Iggy and Gipsy

all lost and in danger, he felt very
lonely indeed.

"What we need is a plan," he said,
gruffly, pulling himself together. "Any
ideas?"

"Eep," said a dimorphodon.

"That's correct," Arx said. "We know
where they're going – Geldos Beta."

"Eep, eep," said another.

"Yes, we *can* go faster than they can,
so we could get there first," he agreed.
"But then what?" He sighed. "Do I
dare risk a rescue? If I mess things up,
Gipsy could get hurt. Oh, if only the
real Teggs and Iggy were here!"

A dimorphodon flapped down and

patted him on the horn with a sympathetic wing.

But then two more of the reptiles squawked. Arx looked up sharply. The sensors were showing a ship close by. "Turn on the scanners!" he barked.

On the screen, Arx could see a small, dark ship approaching. Picked out in red on the side of the craft was a now-familiar dinosaur skull with rows of jagged teeth.

"It's a meat-eater ship," breathed Arx. "And we have no weapons. If they

attack us, we can't fight back!"

The dimorphodon squawked in alarm. Arx started to sweat as the ship drew closer.

"What can I do?" he wailed. "If I run, it means running out on Gipsy. But if I stay, the *Sauropod* could be destroyed. And then the starving dinosaurs on Diplos will *never* get their food in time!"

There was no doubt about it. The carnivore craft was heading straight for the *Sauropod*.

Chapter Eight

DOUBLE-CROSSED!

Arx waited for the approaching ship to ask what he was doing in meat-eater space. He fully expected the rasp of a raptor or the grating roar of a T. rex to sound over the *Sauropod*'s speakers.

But the speakers stayed silent. Had they been damaged in the fight with the death ship?

"If they won't talk to me, I'll have to talk to them," Arx decided. He pressed a button. "Calling carnivore ship.

This is Arx Orano of the DSS *Sauropod*. Can you hear me?"

The ship made no response.

"We are plant-eaters and mean you no harm," said Arx. "We were brought here against our wishes by wanted carnivore criminals. It's a long story. First, we lost our captain and our chief engineer—"

"Cheer up, Arx!" came a hissing voice from the speakers. "You've just found them again!"

"What?" Arx frowned. "Who is this?"

"It's Teggs!" cried the creepy voice.

"And Iggy!" came another, more stupid-sounding voice. "We just worked out how to turn on the communicator!"

"What's happening, Arx?" asked Teggs. "I knew you'd soon see through that dastardly Dasta and his stupid sidekick!"

"Not soon enough, I'm afraid,"

sighed Arx. "Come on board, Captain.
I'll tell you all about it!"

Fifteen minutes later, Teggs was back in
his control pit. He ran around eating
all the ferns he could reach.

Arx looked down at him fondly. "I'm
glad to see that whatever body you're
in, your stomach remains the same
size!"

Teggs grinned up at him. "Just trying
to get the taste of smelly old meat out
of this mouth," he said. "Hey, Iggy,
jump in. Plenty of plants for us both in
here!"

"Incoming!" whooped Iggy, as he dived to join him.

Arx noticed that the dimorphodon were hanging back. They just couldn't believe that these two nasty-looking meat-eaters were actually Teggs and Iggy. But Arx could, now that he'd seen them up close. He could see the friendly sparkle in their eyes. However they looked, that would always stay the same.

"Now then, Arx," Teggs said with a belch. "Let's swap stories."

Teggs told of how he and Iggy had managed to escape rubbish chutes and robots . . . How Iggy had managed to repair the only remaining ship . . . And how they had taken the mind-swapper and headed straight for the Geldos Cluster. They knew Dasta and Ardul would go there, and planned to get their bodies back!

Arx told Teggs of the *Sauropod*'s dangerous journey – and of the one that Gipsy was making even as they spoke. He also explained about Dasta's treasure.

"A replicator?" Iggy frowned. "I don't believe it!"

Arx shrugged. "I wouldn't have believed that a mind-swapping machine was possible – but I'm looking at the proof!"

"Not for much longer, I hope," said Teggs. "Somehow we have to fix Dasta and Ardul for good, set Gipsy free, and swap back into our own bodies."

"And *then* take all those plants and

seeds we're carrying straight to Diplos!" added Arx.

"Is that all?" sighed Iggy. "What shall we do *after* breakfast?"

"Have an early lunch!" Teggs winked at him. "Arx, if we travel at top speed, can we still get to Geldos Beta ahead of Dasta in the shuttle?"

Arx checked with the dimorphodon.

"Just."

"Then let's get moving," Teggs ordered. "I've got a plan — but there's not a moment to lose!"

The *Sauropod* was soon in secret orbit around Geldos Beta. Arx, Iggy and Teggs watched as Dasta's stolen shuttle came into land. Then Teggs and Iggy followed them down in the prison ship at a safe distance.

"We'd better get after them fast," said

Teggs, stepping onto the planet's sandy surface. "As soon as they've got the replicator, they'll take off again."

Iggy nodded grimly. "And that could mean we lose Gipsy as well as the chance to get our bodies back!"

The two transformed astrosaurs scurried off through the sand in search of their real bodies. After a few minutes they reached a sand dune, and climbed to the very top.

"There we are," said Teggs quietly, peeking over the edge. "I mean, there *they* are. We've found them just in time!"

It was a strange feeling, watching themselves.

Dasta, the fake Teggs, was threatening Gipsy with his mighty tail. He swished it about impatiently. Gipsy was digging in the sand, while Ardul half-heartedly helped.

"Ugh," hissed Iggy. "I hate the feeling

of sand between my toes! Watching Ardul do that to my body is giving me shivers!"

"I couldn't stand it if my tail was used to hurt Gipsy," said Teggs softly. "In fact, my plan depends on Gipsy getting well clear of us — I mean, *them*."

Iggy nodded. "What we need is a distraction." Suddenly Ardul jumped high in the air. "We has found it!" he cried, excitedly. "The Sheep-Locator is right here!"

"*Replicator*, you ignoramus!" yelled Dasta. "You're right! There it is! Pull it out, girl, you stripy sausage! I must test it, right away."

Gipsy dragged a large, metal box from out of the sand. It looked like an oven with a big lever on the side and some flashing lights on top. "Doesn't look like much to me," she grunted. "Prepare to be amazed," said Dasta.

Teggs and Iggy watched as he placed a single gold coin inside the replicator and

pulled the lever. The lights flashed
crazily, on and off, on and off – and
then the door swung open.

Gipsy gasped. The
replicator was *bulging*
with gold coins.

"It still works!"
cried Dasta in
delight. He grabbed
some of the coins with his mouth.
"Real gold! Ha! I'm rich! I'm rich!"

"That is where you is wrong," said
Ardul suddenly. He stomped forwards
and picked up the replicator. "Now you
has shown me how this machine works,
I is thinking I shall take it for myself."

"No!" gasped Dasta. "You – you
can't double-cross me!"

"Why not?" asked Ardul.

"Because I was going to double-cross
you first, that's why not!" Dasta raised
his tail. "Now put down the
replicator!"

"No," said Ardul. "I is going to take it away in that shuttle and be rich."

"Over my dead body!" cried Dasta.

Teggs gave Iggy a worried look. "Over *my* dead body, actually!"

"We're not just titchy little coelophysis any more, Ardul," said Dasta. "We're big, mean fighting machines. I could squash you with a swish of this tail!"

Ardul raised his iguanodon thumb
spikes. "Or I could poke you with these
and bring an ear to your tie."

"I think he means a *tear to your eye*,
Dasta," said Gipsy, helpfully.

"I could do that too," Ardul agreed.

"We'll see," snarled Dasta. So saying,
he whacked Ardul on the head with his
tail!

Ardul staggered back and dropped
the replicator on the sand. Then, with
an angry hoot, he charged at Dasta
and knocked him off his feet. Dasta
responded by biting Ardul on the tail.
Ardul yelped, and poked Dasta in the
nose with his sharp thumb.

"Stop fighting, you two!" yelled Gipsy. "You wouldn't treat your own bodies like this, would you?"

"Ouch!" gasped Teggs, as Ardul brought a big rock crashing down on Dasta's head. "We've got to move fast, Iggy – before our bodies are battered to bits. Otherwise we'll be stuck as coelophysis for ever!"

Chapter Nine

A DEADLY GAMBLE

Dasta and Ardul's battle grew wilder. It was stegosaurus versus iguanodon in a furious fighting frenzy!

Ardul jabbed Dasta in the ribs with a karate chop. Dasta gave him a hefty kick with one enormous foot.

The two dinosaurs kept on fighting.
Teggs and Iggy watched in
amazement.

"I didn't know my body could do
that!" gasped Iggy, as Ardul stood on
his hands and slapped Dasta's face with
his short, stiff tail.

"And I didn't know I could balance
on my back!" cried Teggs, as Dasta
spun backwards to get out of the way
and whacked Ardul with his head. "I
have to say, I'm picking up tips!"

"Look!" hissed Iggy. "They're so busy
fighting they've forgotten about Gipsy!"

Gipsy had been left on her own with
the replicator. "Break it up, you two!"
she shouted at Dasta and Ardul. "Those
aren't your bodies to bruise!"

"I'll go and get her," Teggs told Iggy.
"You signal Arx. It's time to put the
plan into action – now!"

With that Teggs raced over the top of

the dune. "Gipsy!" he cried. "Get out of there!"

Gipsy looked up, and gasped. It looked like a mean-looking coelophysis was rushing towards her, teeth bared! Her head-crest flushed red with anger, and she raised her fists, ready for a fight.

"It's all right, Gipsy!" the creature cried. "It's me, Teggs!"

"Teggs?" She peered closely at the scary animal. "Captain, is that really you?"

"Your favourite colour is orange, your mother's name is Doris and you

don't like cabbage,"
cried the coelophysis.

Gipsy grinned. "It *is*
you!"

"It certainly is,"
Teggs agreed. "Now,
pick up that replicator and let's get out
of here. NOW!"

"Yes, sir," she saluted.

Dasta and Ardul were blurs of speed
now as the battle raged on. Tails
thwacked. Heads clunked. Claws
scraped and feet stomped.

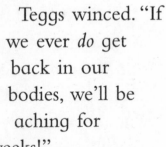

Teggs winced. "If
we ever *do* get
back in our
bodies, we'll be
aching for
weeks!"

Gipsy staggered
along beside him with
the replicator. Then a
dark shadow fell over them.

"The *Sauropod*!" she cried.

Sure enough, the huge, egg-shaped ship was swooping down from the skies above.

"Speed up, Gipsy," Teggs urged her. "We have to put as much distance between us and those carnivore crooks as we can!"

"Why?" panted Gipsy.

"Look out, you two!" cried Iggy. He dashed down and helped them up to the top of the sand dune. "Arx is ready for the big drop!"

"Iggy!" Gipsy dropped the replicator and gave him a massive hug. "Big drop? What do you mean?"

Teggs pointed. "He means *that*!"

The *Sauropod* stopped over the spot where Dasta and Ardul were still fighting. They were so busy bashing each other's brains out, they didn't notice a big pair of doors open above their heads. A second later, tons and

tons of plants and seeds came tumbling out – completely burying the dinosaurs and everything around them!

"Direct hit!" cheered Teggs. "That should stop those stupid crooks fighting for a while!"

"And save our bodies from an even bigger battering!" laughed Iggy.

Dasta's head appeared like a periscope through the sea of seeds. "I'm stuck!" he shouted.

"Me too!" spluttered Ardul, pushing his head out from a pile of plants.

"It's those astrosaurs," Dasta roared. "They've tricked us!"

"True," Teggs agreed with a smile. "Whatever body you're in, it's the *mind* that matters!"

The *Sauropod* landed at the bottom of the sand dune, and Arx came galloping out. Behind him, a flock of dimorphodon flapped about, holding the mind-swapper between them.

"That was a good plan, Captain," Arx smiled. "Now let's get mind-swapping before they dig themselves free!"

The astrosaurs waded through the

scattered seeds and plants to reach
Dasta and Ardul. "It's over, you two,"
said Teggs. "You're going back to your
old bodies – and back to prison!"

Dasta and Ardul struggled but the
food held them firm. The dimorphodon
dropped the helmets on their heads,
while Gipsy looked after Teggs and
Iggy.

"All set, Arx?" asked Teggs hopefully.

But Arx was still peering at the
mind-swapper's controls. "It's more
complicated than I thought it would
be."

"Of course it's complicated! It takes a *genius* to work it," said Dasta proudly. "You haven't a hope!"

Iggy scowled at him. "Tell us how it works!"

"Only if you promise to let me go," said Dasta slyly.

"We can't," Teggs told him. "You're too great a menace. Arx, I'm sorry, but you'll just have to work it out for yourself."

Suddenly Ardul started wiggling about. "While you is doing that, I is going to dig myself free!"

"Quick, Arx," cried Iggy.

"I *think* I can do it," said Arx nervously.

"If you get it wrong, you could fry our minds!" cried Dasta.

"We trust you, Arx," said Teggs. "Do it."

Arx looked at Gipsy. She nodded.

"Very well," he said, his horn hovering over a blue button.

"No!" gasped Dasta. "Not that one!"

"He's trying to trick you, Arx," said Teggs, gritting his teeth. "Do whatever you think is right. That's an order!"

Arx closed his eyes, made a wish and hit the button.

Chapter Ten

WHO'S WHO?!

The mind-swapper hummed and
throbbed and crackled into life. Soon it
was sucking up the dinosaurs' minds
like milkshake.

Teggs gasped. His head felt on fire
again.

Iggy felt the world spinning round and round . . .

"I just hope I've got this machine working properly," said Arx as it rattled and chugged behind him. "What if their minds end up in the wrong bodies? What if they get lost somewhere along the way?"

"You've done your best, Arx," said Gipsy. "Now we just have to hope!"

The mind-swapper sucked harder and harder. The noises it made grew louder and louder. And then it started to smoke. Pink sparks crackled all around it.

"I think it's overloading!" cried Arx. "Get down, Gipsy!"

The two astrosaurs threw themselves

to the ground. The dimorphodon
flapped away into
the sky.

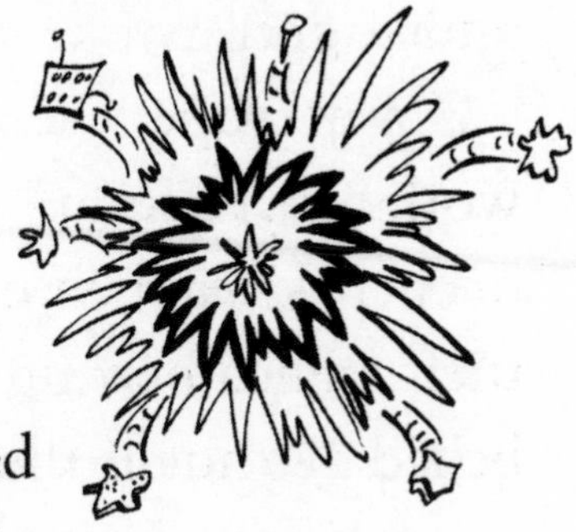

The mind-
swapper throbbed
and spat and
squelched and snorted
. . . And then –

Boom! It exploded in a blaze of light.

"That's that, then," said Arx, getting
back up.

"What if it didn't work?" asked
Gipsy.

"Don't even think that!" he said.

The two coelophysis
were asleep on the
sand. Teggs'
and Iggy's
bodies lay
still, half-
buried by
weeds and
seeds.

Then the stegosaurus stirred. The iguanodon awoke.

Gipsy crossed her hooves. "Teggs? Iggy? Is that you?"

They looked at each other, in a daze.

"I ache all over . . . but I'm back!" yelled Teggs, and he gave a whoop of joy.

"Me too!" cheered Iggy. "We're back in our own bodies!"

"You did it, Arx!" Gipsy hugged him.

"I knew he wouldn't let us down!" beamed Teggs, bounding free of the plants and seeds.

"You're a hero, Arx!" said Iggy. "You deserve a medal!"

Arx blushed.

"Hold on a minute,"

said Teggs. "What about Dasta and
Ardul?"

"Of course!" cried Iggy. "If they're
back in their own bodies, there's
nothing to stop them sneaking off!"

But the astrosaurs were too late. The
two coelophysis had already gone.

"If only I'd watched them," moaned
Gipsy.

The flock of dimorphodon flapped
back down from the sky. One of them
landed on Arx's nose
and gave a loud
squawk.

"This one has
spotted them," said
the triceratops. "He
says they've sneaked
off to your prison ship,
Captain. They'll get away now,
for sure!"

Teggs looked at Iggy and smiled.
"Don't bet on it," he said.

Iggy grinned back. "You see, we left our guard dog on board."

"Guard dog?" Gipsy frowned.

Behind the big sand dune, a clanking, mechanical sound grew slowly louder. Arx and Gipsy cried out as a terrifying monster came into sight.

It was a robot T. rex!

It clutched Dasta in one mighty metal hand and Ardul in the other.

"Don't worry, he's a friend," Iggy explained. "He used to guard the prison, but I rewired him. I needed someone tall to fix the top of the ship!"

"He'll do anything we say," Teggs added. "And he'll certainly hold onto these two until the nearest space prison can pick them up!"

"Curse you, Teggs!" snarled Dasta.

"You is rotten as a raptor!" added Ardul.

"That's a point," said Arx. "We had a

run-in with raptors on the way here. What if we bump into them again on the way back?"

"Don't worry," said Teggs. "Once we've explained how we recaptured two of their most wanted criminals, they'll have to let us leave in peace."

"But what about the starving dinosaurs on Diplos?" asked Gipsy. "What are *they* going to do? We've dumped all their lovely food!"

"Simple," said Iggy. "We give them the replicator!"

Teggs nodded. "Put a single plant into that thing, and ten seconds later . . . out pop a hundred more!"

Arx smiled. "That will solve their food shortage overnight."

"And they'll never be hungry again," said Gipsy. "Brilliant!"

"So what are we waiting for?" said Iggy. "The sooner we deliver it, the better."

He picked up the replicator and set off back to the *Sauropod*. Arx followed, the dimorphodon flapping all around him.

But Gipsy held back. She could see that Teggs was looking at Dasta, still struggling in the grip of the robot T. rex.

"What a waste," he muttered.

Gipsy put a gentle hoof on his shoulder. "You mean . . . if only Dasta had used his brains to help people instead of making himself rich?"

He looked at her, puzzled. "No. I was just thinking – what a *waist*!" He smiled. "That sneaky coelophysis is a real skinny-ribs. It was quite nice to be slim and nimble for a change!"

Gipsy stared at him. "Don't tell me you'd rather be *him* than yourself!"

"No way," cried Teggs, striding off to the *Sauropod* after the others. "I'm the captain of the best ship in the Dinosaur Space Service, with the best crew in the universe. And I must be due another adventure any time now!" He looked back and gave Gipsy an enormous grin. "What could possibly be better than that?"

THE END

TALKING DINOSAUR!

STEGOSAURUS –
STEG-oh-SORE-us

HADROSAUR –
HAD-roh-sore

TRICERATOPS –
try-SERRA-tops

DIMORPHODON –
die-MORF-oh-don

IGUANODON –
ig-WA-noh-don

DIPLODOCUS –
di-PLOH-do-kus

COMPSOGNATHUS –
komp-soh-NAY-thus

COELOPHYSIS –
SEEL-oh-FIE-sis

Astrosaurs

TEETH OF THE T. REX

by
Steve Cole

Illustrated by Woody Fox

RED FOX

For Jill
I would never have got here without you

Chapter One

DINOS IN DISTRESS

The spaceship zoomed past stars and planets on its latest exciting mission.

It was a ship full of dinosaurs! They were all different sizes and all different types. On the flight deck alone there were a stegosaurus, a triceratops, an iguanodon and a stripy hadrosaur, not to mention a flock of dimorphodon

– fifty flying reptiles that worked the ship's switches and levers with their beaks and claws.

The stegosaurus sat chomping on a big clump of grass. His name was Captain Teggs, and the spaceship was called the DSS *Sauropod*. It was the finest ship in the Dinosaur Space Service – with the best-stocked kitchen in the universe. Teggs's favourite things in life were scoffing food and having adventures, and he was always on the look-out for ways to combine the two.

Teggs turned in his control pit to the green triceratops beside him. "Anything to report, Arx?"

"All quiet, Captain," said Arx, Teggs's dinosaur deputy.

Right now they were on border patrol
in the no-man's land between the
Vegetarian Sector – where all the plant-
eaters lived – and the Carnivore Sector,
where no plant-eater would dare set foot!
The sneaky meat-eaters often launched
surprise attacks, and ships like the *Sauropod*
had to stop them.

"Wait!" cried the stripy
hadrosaur, putting
a hoof to her
headphones. Her
name was Gipsy and
she was in charge
of the ship's
communications. "I'm picking
up a mysterious message. I think it's a
distress signal!" Then she gasped and
pulled the headphones away. "Ow! It's
very loud. Ships for millions of miles
around will pick up that message."

Teggs rose up from the control pit. He was as big as a truck, with jagged bony plates running down his orange-brown back. "Quick," he said, "let's hear it through the main speakers."

Gipsy put the signal through – but the second she did, the speakers EXPLODED! The dimorphodon flapped around in fright.

"That's what I call *loud*!" cried Iggy, the iguanodon engineer. "Shall I fix the speakers, Captain? Won't take me a sec."

Teggs nodded. He knew Iggy was brilliant with anything mechanical.

With a last rattle of wires, Iggy finished his repairs. "All done!"

"Play the message again, Gipsy," Teggs said. "Only this time, turn down the volume!"

A gruff female voice burst from the speakers. Even on lowest volume, it shook the flight deck.

"*Um . . . help. Ooooh dear. We is needing, er, helpful dinosaurs to . . . um . . . help us. Come here NOW! Er, please.*"

"That's the message, Captain," said Gipsy. "I've sent a greeting signal but there's no reply."

Teggs frowned. "Whoever they are, it doesn't sound like they're used to asking for help."

"But they're very keen that *someone* hears that message," said Iggy. "That's why the volume's so high."

Arx checked his space radar. "There is a small ship drifting close by. The message must be coming from there."

"Let's see it on the scanner," said Teggs.

A dimorphodon flapped down and pecked the scanner control with his beak. A crumpled grey ship with no markings appeared on the screen, floating beside a large asteroid.

"I've never seen a ship like that before," said Iggy. "Looks like it's been in a crash."

"Still no reply to my signal," said Gipsy.

Teggs rushed to the lift. "Come on, Gipsy, let's check out that ship. Arx, Iggy – stay on full alert till we get back."

The astrosaurs saluted. "Yes, Captain!"

Teggs and Gipsy put on their space armour, just in case of trouble. Then they jumped in a shuttle – one of the six short-range spaceships the *Sauropod* carried – and flew over to the battered ship.

They got inside through a loading bay. The ship's corridors were long and shadowy, and smelled of stale pies and old socks. Gipsy wished she could put a peg on her snout.

"Anyone at home?" Teggs called.

There was no reply.

"Let's go to the control room," Teggs

suggested. "Perhaps we'll find the crew there."

They soon found the control room. The crew weren't there – but something else *was*. A big, bumpy bundle wrapped up in red fur sat on a table in the middle of the room.

"What do you suppose *that* is?" whispered Gipsy.

"Only one way to find out," said Teggs.

He stretched out the tip of his spiky tail and whipped away the red fur. Lying underneath were a wonky golden crown, a gleaming staff shaped like a long claw, a heavy metal chain – and a big bronze skull!

"Yuk!" said Gipsy. "Those things are horrible." Then she noticed a red light flashing on a control panel and went to see. "Captain!" she gasped. "This *machine* sent the distress call. No wonder no one replied to me – it's just a recording!"

But Teggs barely heard her. He had picked up the crown – and found writing scratched into the back. It read:

Thiss krown bellongs to t. rex King
Anywun else touching it will DIE

"Gipsy, these are the T. rex Crown Jewels!" Teggs whispered. "I remember hearing they were stolen from the king's palace last year. He's been searching for them ever since . . ."

Suddenly his communicator bleeped. It was Arx. "Captain, quick!" the triceratops shouted. "A big ship has come out from behind that asteroid and is heading your way. It looks like a carnivore craft – get out of there, fast!"

Teggs gulped. "Come on, Gipsy, back to the shuttle!"

"STAY STILL!" came a deafening roar behind them. "OR US EAT YOU!"

Teggs twirled round to find that four huge scaly nightmares in blood-red uniforms had squeezed inside the control room. Each one was as big as a bungalow with legs as thick as tree-trunks. They had claws like razors and piggy little eyes. Their drooling jaws bristled with knife-sharp teeth the size of bananas.

"Oh, *no!*" Gipsy gulped. "T. rexes!"

Teggs nodded grimly. "We're in trouble now!"

The leader of the monsters stomped towards them. "Us Royal Rex Police," it growled. "You been caught red-handed with our Crown Jewels. Surrender – or DIE!"

Chapter Two

TRIAL BY T. REX

"You are making a mistake," Teggs warned the colossal carnivore, whirling his armoured tail above his head.

But the T. rex leader lunged at him!

Gipsy jabbed it in the leg with her snout, and Teggs whacked it on the end of its nose. It staggered back and knocked over another T. rex. But a third was already pounding over to get them. Gipsy dived forward and skidded underneath its legs, delivering ten judo chops in a single second as she went. With its legs knocked from under it, the T. rex couldn't fight back as Teggs reared up and pushed it over.

But then another of the giant carnivores grabbed Gipsy with its nasty, pinchy claws. "Surrender!" it roared at Teggs. "Or us EAT her."

The bony plates along Teggs's back flushed red with anger. "Watch it, meat-chops!" he snarled. "We are astrosaurs on a mission, answering a distress call. Under Jurassic law sub-section one-point-three paragraph nine – you *can't* eat us."

"Really?" The T. rex looked disappointed. "Oh."

"Lucky you know so much about the law, Captain," hissed Gipsy.

"I don't!" Teggs hissed back. "I just made that up!"

"Us not eat you anyway," sneered the T. rex leader, getting back up and producing two sets of handcuffs. "Us do things proper. You under arrest for stealing."

"But we didn't steal anything!" cried Gipsy as she was roughly cuffed.

The leader ignored her and cuffed Teggs too. "Us take you to our planet, put you on trial and send you to prison," he grunted. "THEN we eat you!"

All the T. rexes roared with nasty laughter as Teggs and Gipsy were dragged struggling away . . .

An hour later, Iggy and the dimorphodon watched helplessly as the police ship took off for the Carnivore Sector with Teggs and Gipsy aboard. The T. rex leader had appeared on the scanner to tell them what had happened – and to warn the *Sauropod* not to follow them.

"This isn't fair!" cried Iggy.

Just then, Arx came back to the flight deck. He looked weary and cross.

"I tried to tell Admiral Rosso about Teggs and Gipsy," said Arx. Rosso was the crusty old barosaurus in charge of the Dinosaur Space Service. "It was no good. He's away on a space expedition and won't be back till late tomorrow."

"But we've got to do something!" Iggy exclaimed.

"I also talked to the T. rex ambassador," Arx went on. "I explained that Teggs and Gipsy were tricked into going aboard that ship by a fake distress call. I said that the Crown Jewels must have been placed there for them to find. I pointed out what a coincidence it was that there just happened to be a Royal Rex Police ship close by. And I urged him to set Teggs and Gipsy free so we can help find the *real* villains."

Iggy nodded eagerly. "What did he say?"

"He burped, made a rude noise with his bottom and fell asleep!" Arx sighed. "You just can't reason with a T. rex."

"So what happens to Teggs and Gipsy now?" asked Iggy.

Arx looked worried. "They will be sent to Claw Court on the planet Teerex Major."

"Good," said Iggy. "The judge will soon see they are innocent."

"I'm not so sure," said Arx. "This trial will be led by Judge Braxus the Bloodthirsty – the toughest, meanest judge in the entire Jurassic Quadrant!"

Teggs and Gipsy huddled together in the middle of the T. rex Claw Court. It was a large, dark building that stank of rotten meat and armpits. Bones and bloodstains covered the floor. Sitting all around were jeering, drooling T. rexes who had come to watch the trial. Each was as tall as three elephants, and the astrosaurs felt very small in comparison.

"I wish they had let us keep our armour," said Teggs. "I feel naked without it!"

"I wish Arx was allowed to defend us," Gipsy said sadly.

"He'd get us off just like that!" Teggs agreed. "Unlike our useless lump of a lawyer there."

A T. rex in a little grey wig was sitting to one side. She was supposed to be sticking up for them today – but since she had already tried to eat them twice in the last half-hour, Teggs wasn't sure her heart was really in it.

"All stand!" someone growled. "Here come Judge Braxus!"

The watching crowd jumped up, roaring and cheering, as a squat, ugly T. rex in red robes and a bloodstained wig swaggered inside and perched on a tall chair. "Silence in court!" he shouted. "Or me kill you!"

The courtroom fell silent.

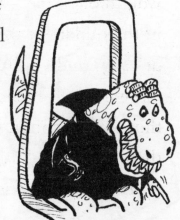

"Hey, you! Astrosaur scumballs!" said Braxus. "How does you bleed?"

"You mean, 'How do you *plead*?'," Teggs corrected him.

Braxus grinned nastily. "Me know what me means."

Gipsy turned to their lawyer. "Are you going to let him threaten us like that?"

But their lawyer was snoring. She had fallen asleep!

"Where is first witness?" called Braxus.

The Royal Rex Police leader forced his way through the jostling crowd and stood in the middle of the courtroom, glaring at Teggs and Gipsy. "Us got tip-off that Crown Jewels hidden on that ship – and that thieves coming there to collect them," he said. "Us come looking."

"But we were tricked into going

there," said Teggs. "We were answering a distress call that turned out to be a rotten recording! Whoever tipped you off must have left the Crown Jewels on that ship and used a fake distress call to lure us on board – knowing that you would find us!"

"Rubbish," shouted Judge Braxus. "Me find you GUILTY!"

"That's not fair!" cried Gipsy.

But the crowd went wild. "*Guilty! Guilty!*" they chanted in delight. They made such a din that even the astrosaurs' lawyer was woken up.

"Objection!" she spluttered.

"Me EAT anyone who objects," Braxus warned her.

The lawyer turned to Teggs and Gipsy. "Bye," she grunted – and ran for it!

"Me find astrosaur scumballs VERY guilty," Braxus went on. "You be sent to Saint Bonecracker's Prison – worst prison on Teerex Major."

"You can't do this to us!" Teggs shouted.

"Can so too!" Braxus retorted. "Me send you there for ten years – but you probably be eaten in ten MINUTES. Ha, ha, ha!"

The judge's laughter mingled with the howls and shrieks of the T. rex hordes all around them. Gipsy and Teggs hugged each other as the racket rocked Claw

Court to its foundations. "We've been in some tight scrapes before, Gipsy," said Teggs grimly. "But never as tight as *this*!"

Chapter Three

PRISONERS!

Teggs and Gipsy were booted out of Claw Court and chucked into a T. rex police shuttle. It took them straight to St Bonecracker's prison, an enormous towering castle that looked as dark and scary as a hundred haunted houses rolled into one.

Inside it was no better. The smell of sweaty claws and dirty bottoms filled the air. The warders were huge, clanking robots that fired laser beams from their eyes if anyone misbehaved. Teggs and Gipsy had to take off their astrosaur uniforms and wear nasty grey prison outfits, stained with things Teggs didn't like to think about.

Then the robots took the new arrivals to report to the prison governor – Mrs Fangetta.

"Welcome to my prison, plant-eating scum!" growled Fangetta. She was warty and extremely ugly. Around her waist she wore a shabby tutu that was the same sickly pink colour as her eyes.

"Me not think you like it here much!"

Gipsy gave her a hard stare. "When the Dinosaur Space Service hears about this, you're going to be in big trouble."

"Unless you let us go now," Teggs added hopefully.

Fangetta started laughing. "Let you go? That a good one." She tried to hold her ribs, but her feeble arms weren't quite long enough. "Ha ha ha, my sides is splitting!"

Suddenly Teggs noticed a framed photo on Fangetta's desk. It was a picture of her cuddling Braxus the Bloodthirsty!

"I see you know our judge," he remarked.

At once, Fangetta stopped laughing. Her pink eyes narrowed. "Braxus send many crooks here. Him decent, upstanding T. rex."

Gipsy stared at her. "But he's a bonkers, bloodthirsty maniac!"

"To a T. rex, that *is* decent and upstanding," Teggs reminded her.

"Me not have you talk about my lickle Braxie-waxie like this," she roared, thwumping her tail against the floor so hard that the door of the cupboard behind her fell open – to reveal something surprising.

"Hang on," said Gipsy. "Aren't those the Crown Jewels we're supposed to have stolen?"

"Yes!" Teggs frowned. "How come *you've* got them?"

Fangetta looked suddenly shifty. "Um . . . This be prison. Good place to lock things up safe. Me guarding the jewels till King Groosum get here."

"The T. rex ruler is coming *here*?" said Gipsy, the crest on her head flushing blue with alarm.

"Yeah!" Fangetta gave her a nasty smile. "Him want to meet you. Him want to teach you lesson you never forget. Then us hold special feast in his honour, and give him back Crown Jewels."

"Sounds fun," joked Teggs. "What a shame we won't be able to go."

"Maybe you will," said Fangetta

mysteriously. "Warders, take them to
their cells – before me eats them
NOW!"

Gipsy and
Teggs looked
at each other
helplessly as
the robots
clanked back
into the room
and yanked
them away . . .

Back on the *Sauropod*, Arx and Iggy
were waiting tensely for Admiral Rosso
to get back from his space expedition.

"I just don't get it," said Iggy. "Why
did whoever stole the Crown Jewels
suddenly want to get rid of them?"

"Maybe the jewels were just too risky
to keep," said Arx. "With thousands of

angry T. rex police tearing space apart for them, wouldn't *you* hand them over?"

"But why not just dump them on that ship?" Iggy wondered. "Why bother to frame someone else for the crime?"

"I don't know," said Arx. "But I know of one T. rex in particular who'll be pleased – Thickhead McBrick!"

Iggy frowned. "Who?"

"He was accused of stealing the Crown Jewels," Arx explained. "He never admitted it, but they chucked him in prison anyway. Now I suppose they'll have to let him go." He paused. "Funnily enough, he was sent to Saint Bonecracker's Prison by Braxus the Bloodthirsty too – just like Teggs and Gipsy."

"I hate to think of them in that terrible place!" cried Iggy. "Arx, we can't wait any longer for Admiral Rosso. We have to get them out of prison!"

"We can't take a DSS ship into the Carnivore Sector when the T. rexes warned us not to. It could start an intergalactic war!" said Arx. Then he smiled. "However – if the two of us went in a small, unmarked ship . . ."

"Of course!" Iggy cheered. "The battered old ship that started all this is just outside! We can travel in that!"

"Come on, then," said Arx, charging to the lift. "If we're going to save our friends, there's no time to lose!"

It was lunchtime back in St Bonecrackers, and Teggs and Gipsy were sitting in a quiet corner of the prison canteen. They stared miserably at their untouched bowls of maggot-

and-tailbone stew.

"I'm starving!" Teggs groaned. "You'd think this restaurant would have a vegetarian option!"

"Not when everyone else is a meat-eater," said Gipsy. She looked up from her bowl and gulped. "Uh-oh. Looks like one or two of our fellow inmates think *we* look tastier than this sloppy stew . . ."

Teggs turned and gasped. "One or two *hundred*, you mean!"

While the robot warders looked the other way, drooling T. rexes had sneaked up and surrounded them! Claws twitched and jaws snapped open and shut as the gigantic carnivores closed in on the astrosaurs . . .

Chapter Four

TUNNEL OF FEAR

"I'll hold them off," said Teggs bravely as the T. rexes lumbered closer. "Gipsy, get ready to run."

But Gipsy shook her head. "No way! If this is the end, we will face it together!"

But then help came from an unexpected source – Teggs's stomach!

RROOAAARRR! Teggs was so hungry that his tummy rumbled and growled like there were fifty ravenous raptors trapped inside! The extraordinary noise echoed around the canteen.

"Excuse me," said Teggs, rubbing his empty belly. But the T. rexes had stopped. They were watching him with fear in their eyes.

"Me never hear roar as scary as that before!" one said.

"Quick, Captain, do it again!" Gipsy urged him.

"I can't just make my tummy rumble!" he hissed back at her.

"You can! Think of a big bowl of fern falafels and carrot custard and juicy leaf risotto . . ."

Teggs did – and this time his stomach rumbled like an earthquake kicking off. *RRRRROOOOAAAAAARRRRR!*

The T. rexes backed away in alarm. "Us not eating big growly thing like that!" they shouted, smashing into tables and squashing their chairs as they rushed to get away.

The robot warders
finally looked up at
all the ruckus going
on, and started
blasting at the crowd
with their eye lasers.
"STAND STILL OR DIE!"

Even the stupidest
T. rexes understood that
order, and did as they were told.

Two robot warders clanked over to
the astrosaurs and grabbed them by the
tails. "YOU ARE TROUBLEMAKERS," it
droned. "WE WILL TAKE YOU TO MRS
FANGETTA FOR PUNISHMENT."

"Can't wait." Teggs sighed.

The robots dragged them off to
Fangetta's office. Someone was just
coming out – a stooped, skinny T. rex
who was nasty looking even by
carnivore standards.

"Goodbye, Thickhead McBrick!" called Fangetta. "Congratulations on your release!"

"Ha!" Thickhead sniggered. "And me owe it all to you astrosaurs!"

"What are you on about?" asked Gipsy.

"Me was put in here 'cause they thought me stole Crown Jewels," said Thickhead. "Now King knows *you* did it, me has been given royal pardon. Me free!" He danced off down the corridor. "So long, suckers!"

Teggs scowled. "You know, what *really* bugs me about all this is that the real Crown Jewel thief is still at large."

"Don't talk stupid," hissed Fangetta, stomping out of her office in her grimy tutu. "Everyone knows YOU done it. Now, what you doing back here already?"

"PRISONERS CAUSED TROUBLE IN CANTEEN," said one of the warders.

"Oh dear, dear," said Fangetta, with a nasty smile. "This means PUNISH-MENT. Me send you to kitchens."

Teggs groaned. "You mean we have to help make your repulsive meaty meals?"

"Me not send you to work." Fangetta smiled. "Me send you to STEWPOT!

Your punishment is to be king's dinner at royal feast tonight. Mmm, astrosaur stew – delicious!" She licked her leathery lips, splashing drool over the floor. "Take them away!"

"You monsters!" cried Gipsy, struggling furiously against the metal grip of the warders as she and Teggs were dragged off to the kitchens . . .

Meanwhile, Arx and Iggy had reached Teerex Major in the unmarked spaceship. Arx checked his guide book. "It says that Saint Bonecracker's is in the smelliest, noisiest, dirtiest district on the planet," he reported. "I expect T. rexes are queuing up to live around there!"

They landed in a parking bay close to the prison. Iggy had brought some power tools with him. "The easiest way to get Teggs and Gipsy out of jail is to dig a tunnel," he explained. "We must dig one right under the prison walls, find them and escape back here."

"I've got a plan of the prison," said Arx, waving a piece of paper. "That should make sure we don't come out in the middle of a T. rex cell!"

They peeped out of the spaceship. The air smelled of rotten meat and old dung. Rocket-cars and space trains made a terrible racket all around. T. rex traffic wardens patrolled the bay, handing out tickets – and eating anyone who complained!

Arx and Iggy sneaked out when the
wardens weren't looking and hid
underneath the little ship. Then they
started to dig their tunnel. Iggy had a
super-spade and Arx used a power-
pickaxe. No one could hear them
working over the din of the
traffic, and soon they
were making good
progress through
the dark
slimy mud.

"Let's aim for the prison library," suggested Arx, checking the map. "That should be nice and quiet – none of the T. rexes can actually read!"

"And it's not too far from the cell blocks either," Iggy noted. "Come on!"

But suddenly the roof of the tunnel began to tremble above them.

"Look out!" cried Arx. "The mud must be crumblier here. This whole section of the tunnel is going to cave in on top of us!"

"No time to go back," Iggy shouted as heavy soil started raining down about them. "We'll just have to keep going forward!"

The stocky iguanodon swung the super-spade with all his strength, faster and faster as the tunnel roof crashed down behind him. He made his tunnel slope upwards so less mud could fall in on them, digging and digging until he'd lost all track of time. Finally, once he was certain the roof above was secure, Iggy collapsed in a sweaty heap.

"Phew," he said. "That was a close one, wasn't it, Arx?"

No reply.

"Arx?" he repeated.

But Arx wasn't there!

"Oh no," groaned Iggy. "We've been cut off by the cave-in!" He yelled down the tunnel. "Arx? You'd better not be squashed flat under all that mud! Where are you?"

"WHO THAT DOWN THERE?" came a scary shout from just beyond the tunnel roof.

"Uh-oh," said Iggy, with a sinking feeling. "I don't know where I am – but I must have dug myself back up to ground level!"

Suddenly, huge scaly feet came smashing through the tunnel roof, and nasty claws reached down to yank him out of the ground. Blinking in the bright light, too exhausted from digging to run, Iggy found himself surrounded by ugly meat-eaters in scruffy dinner suits. Clunky robots were offering drinks and raw meat to the guests – and one of those robots was holding him by the tail in an unbreakable grip.

"Um . . . great party!" Iggy smiled weakly at the snarling faces all around.

"I always like to make a big entrance . . ."

Then an ugly female T. rex in a pink tutu and tiara pushed through the crowd. She was holding hands with a squat, ugly male in red robes and a bloodstained wig. "Look, Braxus!" she cried, an evil smile spreading over her face. "Us found uninvited iguanodon. Look like *another* astrosaur!"

"Him must be here to save his criminal friends, Fangetta," said Braxus. "Instead, him will join them – ON OUR DINNER PLATES!"

Chapter Five

ASTROSAUR STEW!

Teggs and Gipsy had been tied up with
rope and squashed together in a big

cauldron. It stood
in the corner of
the prison's
grandest dining
room – a
damp, rotten
place filled
with rickety
tables and
chairs. Beneath
the cauldron was a big pile of firewood,
ready to be lit.

"I wish the T. rex chef had added more potatoes to this salty water," said Teggs as he gulped the last one down. Eating helped to take his mind off the grisly fate that awaited them. "Some swampgrass would be nice too – to really bring out our full flavour."

Gipsy forced a brave smile. She knew Teggs was only joking to keep her spirits up. "Oh, Captain, I can't believe we're going to end up in a T. rex's tum!" she cried. "If only we could get out of here—"

Suddenly the dining-room door burst open.

"Iggy!" cried Gipsy, who couldn't believe her eyes.

Teggs cheered. "He's come to save us!"

"Er . . . sorry, guys," said Iggy. And

now Gipsy could see Fangetta and Braxus standing right behind him. "I got caught."

"Soon us light fire beneath you," growled Fangetta. "Then you be HOT DINNER!" She and Braxus tied Iggy up tight and plopped him into the pot.

"Thanks for trying to save us, Ig," said Gipsy fondly. "But where's Arx?"

"I don't know," Iggy admitted. "The tunnel we were digging fell in on us. We got split up." He sniffed. "I don't even know if he's still alive!"

Gipsy gasped with horror, and Teggs bowed his head. Things had never seemed more desperate. He glared at their carefree carnivore captors as they fussed over who would sit where at the royal feast.

"This where King Groosum gonna be," said Fangetta, pointing to a grotty throne. "You go on one side, me go on other side. Thickhead McBrick sit on next table."

"Thickhead?" Teggs frowned. "What's he doing here?"

"Maybe the king wants to say sorry for locking him up," said Gipsy. "After all, he thinks *we* are the real crooks now."

"When do us give King the Crown Jewels?" asked Braxus, pointing to the large red fur bundle in front of the throne.

"As soon as him come in," said Fangetta. Then she sniggered. "Us not want him to think us want to hang on to Crown Jewels . . ."

"No, us would not want him thinking that," Braxus agreed, joining in the laughter.

"What's so funny?" wondered Iggy. "Are they up to something?"

"I don't know," Gipsy admitted. "What do you think, Captain?"

"I think," Teggs spluttered as he pulled his head out from the salty water, "that the spaghetti they put in this stew is really, really tough!" Even so, he took a deep breath and ducked his head back under to go on chewing.

Suddenly a robot warder crashed into the dining room. "GUESTS ARE READY TO ENTER," it droned.

"COME IN, THEN!" Fangetta hollered.

Gipsy watched nervously as sixty rowdy T. rexes came piling into the room, squabbling and fighting over who sat where. Thickhead McBrick made his way through the scaly scrum and sat down close to Fangetta. He winked at her, and she winked back.

"Those two seem surprisingly friendly," murmured Gipsy.

But Teggs seemed more interested in his last supper. "This spaghetti isn't just tough, it tastes revolting!" he spluttered, coming up for air. "But I'm so hungry I could eat *anything* . . ."

Meanwhile, Braxus had battled his way over to the main doors. "Stop fighting, you lot!" he shouted at the guests. "Welcome His Royal Nastiness . . . King Groosum the Great!"

Gipsy and Iggy gulped as Braxus led the king inside and everyone clapped and cheered. King Groosum was massive, taller and scarier than any T. rex they had ever seen – very nearly the size of a house! He wore dirty purple robes and a necklace of dinosaur skulls around his fat, blubbery neck. He roared in the guests' faces and whacked them with his tail, and they loved it.

At last the king reached his throne. "Sorry me late," he said. "Me just taken someone's hand in marriage." He pulled a gory claw from under his cloak and waved it around. "BUT ME NO LIKE THE REST OF HER!"

The room shook with laughter as King Groosum swallowed the claw and burped loudly. Then Fangetta stood up and cleared her throat. "And now us would like to present His Royal Nastiness with his long-lost treasure!"

Braxus threw back the red fur covering the Crown Jewels, and everyone gasped in wonder. King Groosum gave a contented sigh as he placed the crown upon his head.

Everyone clapped once more – but Braxus called for silence. "And now, to celebrate getting back jewels, us watch stealing astrosaur scum BOIL ALIVE in our big stewpot . . ."

Teggs splashed his head out from under the salty water. "What did he say?"

Braxus pointed to one of the robot warders. "Light the fire!"

"I wish I hadn't asked!" said Teggs.

The robot clanked towards them, aiming its lasers at the firewood beneath the cauldron . . .

Chapter Six

THE TOOTH REVEALED!

"That was a rubbish last meal," complained Teggs as the robot warder clanked closer. But there was a sparkle in his eyes. "Gipsy, do I have something stuck between my teeth?"

"Hang on!" Gipsy stared at a thick strand hanging out of his mouth. "That's not spaghetti . . . it's *rope!*"

Iggy gasped. "You just chewed through the ropes they tied us up with!"

"I *told* you I was hungry enough to eat anything!" Teggs beamed. "I just didn't want to get you excited in case I couldn't free us in time."

"But you have," said Gipsy, narrowing her eyes at the gigantic, slavering T. rexes. "Which is bad news for this lot!"

"I'm ready for some action," Iggy agreed heartily.

"And this swimming pool of theirs is a bit cramped," said Teggs. "So how about we—?"

"BREAK OUT!" they all shouted together. And before the robot could fire its lasers, all three astrosaurs sprang out of the cauldron, propelled by their tails!

Teggs landed feet first on Fangetta, squashing her into the floor. Then he whacked Braxus in the belly with his spiky tail. The T. rex staggered backwards and knocked into King Groosum – who almost swallowed his staff as he toppled off the throne!

Gipsy landed on Thickhead's table. The skinny crook tried to bite her leg, but she leaped over his head and jabbed him in the back of the neck. He was sent sprawling, knocking over nearby guests like giant skittles.

Iggy landed in the arms of the robot warder. He stuck his thumb spikes into its metal head and sent it haywire! The robot began to jerk about, and T. rexes dived for cover as it started firing laser beams all over the place.

"OK, astrosaurs," Teggs shouted. "Let's get out of here!"

Iggy and Gipsy didn't need telling

twice. They raced after their captain, dodging laser beams and slashing claws and dripping jaws. And they had almost reached the exit when a familiar figure appeared in the doorway.

"Arx!" cheered Teggs. "You're alive!"

"EVERYONE STOP WHERE THEY ARE!" Arx thundered.

He sounded so angry and powerful, the T. rexes did as they were told!

"Come on, Arx," hissed Iggy. "Don't push your luck, let's get going."

"We can't run away now," said the triceratops. "If we do, Captain Teggs and Gipsy will stay wanted criminals for ever."

"That because them ARE wanted criminals!" roared King Groosum through a mouthful of staff.

"No!" Arx shouted, waving a golden,

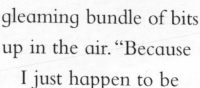

gleaming bundle of bits up in the air. "Because I just happen to be holding the *real* T. rex Crown Jewels! Your Majesty, those ones you've been given are FAKES!"

Teggs and Gipsy gasped. Iggy's jaw dropped. Most of the T. rexes looked confused.

But Braxus, Fangetta and Thickhead looked at each other and said: "Uh-oh!"

"A few hours ago I was digging a tunnel beneath the prison," Arx went on. "The tunnel roof caved in and I only just managed to dig myself out. I emerged in the middle of Mrs Fangetta's office, and found these treasures stuffed in her cupboard." He marched up to King Groosum and placed them in front of him. "See?"

Fangetta, looking a bit squashed, sneered at Arx. "You lie! *Them* the fakes!"

"No!" growled King Groosum, plucking half a staff from his mouth. "Me chew my staff many times. It never taste as cheap and muck-worthy as this." He grabbed Arx's staff and nibbled the end. "Yes! This REAL staff! Me recognize my toothmarks!"

Thickhead, Fangetta and Braxus all started to run – but Teggs, Iggy and Gipsy tripped them up. They fell flat on their faces and the astrosaurs sat on their backs to hold them down.

"These three greedy T. rexes tried to trick us all," Arx explained.

"But how?" asked Teggs. "What's been going on?"

"Confess, Thickhead," Gipsy warned him. "Or I'll jab you somewhere you won't like!"

"All right." Thickhead sighed. "Me really *did* steal Crown Jewels from King's palace. And me hide them good."

"But you couldn't sell them while you were stuck in prison," said Arx. "So you did a deal with Mrs Fangetta, didn't you? You said that she and her boyfriend, Braxus, could share the loot with you in exchange for your freedom!"

Thickhead nodded. "It be true."

"Oh, *I* get it now!" said Teggs angrily. "For you to go free, someone else had to be found guilty."

"And that meant framing them with a fake set of jewels," Gipsy added. "So you could go off and sell the real ones later!"

Braxus glared at Thickhead. "Whatever you do, do not tell them that unmarked spaceship was mine, or that me tipped off the Royal Rex Police about where to find it – or else!"

"Or that me made the fake jewels and done the distress call," said Fangetta quickly.

"You dino-dimwits!" Iggy yelled. "You just told us yourselves!"

"Oh no!" wailed Fangetta and Braxus. He covered her mouth and she covered his, while the other T. rexes laughed and jeered at them.

Then King Groosum
reared up to his full,
horrifying height
and looked down at
the astrosaurs. "It
look like me must thank
you for finding real Crown Jewels.
So – me will not eat you."

Teggs gave him a crooked smile.
"How generous!"

"Me let you all go free," King
Groosum declared grandly. "But these
three tricksters be staying right here in
prison for very, VERY long time."

Gipsy, Teggs and Iggy jumped up
from their fallen foes as robot warders
came to take the T. rex trio to the cells.

"Astrosaur scum!" snarled Fangetta.

"We get you for this!" Braxus roared.

"Don't think so, Judge," laughed Teggs.
"You've been well and truly *court* out!"

Kicking and struggling, Braxus, Fangetta and Thickhead were hauled away . . .

Teggs and Gipsy changed back into their uniforms and then joined the others in the little unmarked ship in the parking bay. Iggy wasted no time blasting off into the smoggy skies of Teerex Major.

"Yay!" Gipsy gave Teggs a hug. "We are free!"

Teggs beamed. "Thanks to Arx and Iggy."

"We make a good team," Iggy agreed.

Arx nodded happily. "Now, let's get back to the *Sauropod* where the *rest* of the team is waiting."

Teggs smiled. "Not only them," he said. "I'll bet new adventures – massive jumbo *T. rex*-sized adventures – are waiting for us too!"

And so the astrosaurs sped off through the stars to find them.

THE END

READ ON FOR
BRAND-NEW
ASTRO-FILES!

ASTRO-FILES

SUBJECT: Captain Teggs Horatio Stegosaur

AGE: 25

PLANET OF HATCHING: Steggos

HISTORY: Teggs hatched from his egg on the first day of the space year 37 million. His mum and dad were swamp farmers who mainly grew ferns (which fast became Teggs's favourite food – along with gravity grapes and Christmas trees).

Growing up, Teggs bought bundles of books and taped hundreds of TV shows about the Dinosaur Space Service. He soon became an expert, and passed the entrance exam to Astrosaurs Academy with flying colours. Here he made friends with loads of astrosaur cadets, such as Dutch Delaney, Blink Fingawing, Damona Furst, Netta Arinetta and Linford Splatt.

Teggs helped save the Academy from a variety of deadly dangers, and always took great care of his friends and fellow cadets – risking his life for theirs without hesitation. By the end of his first year he had won more medals than any other cadet in astrosaur history.

As part of his final space exam, Teggs invented the Dung-Dump Manoeuvre. When faced with a Raptor Death Ship about to open fire with all lasers, Teggs dumped all his dung torpedoes directly in the path of the raptor ship. The torpedoes went off together in one big bang and transformed the carnivore craft into a massive, smelly dung ball!

DSS head Admiral Rosso made Teggs captain of his own spaceship just days later. That spaceship was the DSS *Sauropod*, one of the finest ships in the universe. And Teggs started his life as an astrosaur in super-cool style when he and his crew saved the Great Dinosaur Games on Olympus from the evil of General Loki and his raptors.

CONCLUSION: Teggs is one of the best-loved (and hungriest!) astrosaurs in the DSS. He has won enough medals to completely cover the neck of a diplodocus, and has eaten several planets' worth of ferns. Long may his adventures continue!

ASTRO-FILES

SUBJECT: Communications Officer Gipsy Saurine

AGE: 21

PLANET OF HATCHING: Corythos

HISTORY: Gipsy is the youngest of fifteen hadrosaur hatchlings. Her mother worked in the Dinosaur Space Service and had jobs on many different planets. As a result, Gipsy grew up hearing many languages, and soon found she was able to learn them in record time. Gipsy liked to help her mum by taking messages when the astro-assistants were at lunch – however tricky or tongue-twisting they were, she repeated them word-for-word every time.

Her mum's friends in the DSS encouraged her to send Gipsy to a private Astrosaur Communications School on Corytho to develop her skills. Since she was so used to travelling between planets, Gipsy asked if she could work on spaceships once she passed her astrosaur exams. Her first job was as Communications Assistant on the DSS *Lizard Queen*. After several adventures patrolling the Vegmeat Zone – fighting raptors, space-snakes and the Giant Squelchy Eyeballs of the Doom-Dust Cluster as she did so – Gipsy was promoted to Communications Officer on board the brand-new *Sauropod*.

Gipsy is highly skilled in eleven martial arts including dino-judo, tailspin-X and hoof-jab-a-go-go. Although she dislikes weapons, she is very skilled with a sword as she once demonstrated during a run-in with some star pirates. In common with all hadrosaurs born on Corytho, Gipsy's head-crest changes colour according to how she is feeling – blue if she is alarmed, green if she feels sick, purple if puzzled or deep red if she is angry.

CONCLUSION: Growing up in such a large family, Gipsy learned the importance of fair play and of caring for others – qualities that have served her well as an astrosaur. Clever and cool, with a sunny personality, Gipsy is an indispensable member of the *Sauropod* crew.

ASTRO-FILES

SUBJECT: Chief Engineer Iggadoo Tooth

AGE: 26

PLANET OF HATCHING: Iguanos

HISTORY: Iggadoo (known as 'Iggy' or 'Ig' to his friends) was brought up in one of the poorest areas of the iguanodon planet. His father worked day and night as a mechanic, repairing all kinds of vehicles. Iggy spent most of his early years helping out in his dad's workshop.

Iggy showed amazing skill. In less than twelve months he went from cleaning the floors to stripping down jet-cycle engines single-handed. During this time he also got into robotics, and began using the odds and ends lying around the workshop to invent incredible new machines (almost blowing up his house on more than one occasion!).

But it was only when his dad was hired by a moon-shuttle company that young Iggy realized he wanted to become a spaceship engineer. He spent every night in his dad's garage tinkering with the shuttles while studying spacecraft designs. The owner of the moon-shuttle company, a retired astrosaur, was so impressed he got Iggy a job in the DSS Solar Workshops near Lambeos.

Iggy now found himself working on gigantic spaceship engines, doing his astrosaur exams in his spare time. His bosses saw that he was able to fix almost any machine – usually making it better at the same time. So when barosaurus boffins drew up plans for the finest ship in the astrosaur fleet – the DSS *Sauropod* – Iggy was asked to help. He built the brakes and helped install the engines – and did such a good job he was made the *Sauropod*'s Chief Engineer.

CONCLUSION: Whether keeping up spirits with a silly song or turning a clawful of scrap into a vital piece of enemy-bashing machinery, Iggy is a mega-cool member of the *Sauropod* team – brave, tough and loyal to the end!

ASTRO-FILES

SUBJECT: First Officer Arx Longhorn Orano

AGE: 52

PLANET OF HATCHING: Tri Major

HISTORY: Arx hatched from his egg in an underground station during a bombing raid in the first days of the T. rex–Triceratops War. Eighteen years later, Arx became the youngest ever pilot of a triceratops star-cruiser, capturing over 200 enemy ships. After the war, Arx turned down a job with the DSS so he could stay on Tri-Major and help to rebuild the planet.

Over the next few years, he invented several new